Celebrant Sleuth

HAZEL EDWARDS

Published by BookPOD

Cover artwork © 2017 Lee Burgemeestre

A Catalogue-in-Publication is available from the National Library of Australia.

ISBN: 978-1-925457-71-1
eISBN: 978-1-925457-72-8

Contents

About the Author

Hazel Edwards OAM has published 200 books including 'There's a Hippopotamus on Our Roof Eating Cake' classic series currently touring as 'Hippo Hippo the Musical', 'Hijabi Girl' co-written with Muslim librarian Ozge Alkan about a feisty 8 year old who wants to start a girls' footy team, is her latest junior book. A cultural risk-taker, Hazel co-wrote 'f2m: the boy within' a YA novel about trans youth. A believer in participant-observation research, Hazel has been an Antarctic expeditioner. She mentors 'Hazelnuts' writers and was on the Australian Society of Authors board. 'Not Just a Piece of Cake: Being an Author' is her memoir based on anecdultery as a creative structure. Her books have been translated in ten languages and adapted for other mediums. 'Difficult Personalities' (PRH) co-written with Dr Helen Mc Grath is available in Russian, Polish, Korean, Chinese, American and audio. Currently writing adult mysteries including 'Almost a Crime'. www.hazeledwards.com

Quinn–Introducing Myself

I married my sister and buried my father.

And I'm guilty of using that opening line a few times.

To attract attention? Maybe.

I'm a celebrant.

I perform ceremonies like weddings and funerals.

But I have other roles too:

The inadvertent sleuth, and problem-solver, that's me.

Since I'm a romantic, I like everybody to be emotionally satisfied at the ceremony, and afterwards. I love to see the beefy, muscled truck driver with the tats get a bit weepy as his new petite bride in her lacy dress and hi-hi red heels cuts the decorated, red wedding cake, the one he made. Atypicals find each other and survive as a couple even if outsiders can't see why. Like Art and me. No one, especially his parents, thought we'd survive seven years. Who ever knows for sure? I don't, but occasionally the clues are there.

At funerals, my heart goes out to genuinely bereaved partners who are stunned by the loss of the person who reflects their private, best self. So I help by celebrating that life-story and recording the memories as a eulogy. I prefer funerals to weddings despite the shorter notice. Even if there is a close deadline (such an unfortunate word) to write the ceremony, when it has been a long life and well lived, there's a satisfaction in creating the eulogy as a tribute.

That's my job.

I celebrate, and orchestrate, special occasions.

Sometime they want a male celebrant. Others prefer a woman. I get a lot of work. I'm adaptable. I'm also reliable, turn up on time and have an actor's voice which can be heard by deaf, elderly relatives who refuse out of vanity to wear their expensive, hearing aids.

Plus I write the 'dreaded' eulogy if requested. At first I was surprised families didn't feel skilled or confident enough to write their own genuine tributes, but then I started to like that role best, as the creative part. Like composing a mini-history of motives and why they became that person in those times. Sort of high level gossip. Mainly the good bits, but hint at the rest. We all have secret lives, and secrets and maybe some need to be shared on significant occasions.

Do I have secrets? Of course.

But I'm not secretive about my gender, it just isn't relevant much of the time.

Gender is a funny thing. I think my gender is 'shrug'. I mean, I don't particularly feel any gender, I find it hard to wrap my head around the concept that most people implicitly feel male or female or something else. Possibly that makes me agender, but I really don't feel it strongly enough to care. So people use female pronouns for me and that's fine, because 'shrug', I'm just Quinn.

To an outsider, Art and I look like a conventional couple, (except he is shorter) and I'm formally dressed in a themed-with-the-bride coloured jacket as a female celebrant when I'm working. Red, purple (most popular with brides) or blue with reversible cuffs to look different in the photos for the website later. Not forgetting the black jacket for funerals. Or t-shirt, sneakers and jeans other times. I prefer ice cream to sex, but I'm still a romantic and have feelings and attachments.

'I married my sister and buried my father.'

Strictly speaking, that's true too. My Dad wanted me to do his farewell ceremony. And partly why I started as a celebrant for weddings and funerals. I performed both those ceremonies for my family just after I qualified. Quite emotional inside but I managed by using my actor voice and 'playing the role' of celebrant.

Really loved my Dad. So it was a challenge not to let the tears take over when I realised it was so final. Or to be so choked up, I couldn't get the words out to do him credit. But afterwards, I felt I'd done my best for him. Even if I got the exit music wrong. But he did like 'When the Saints Go Marching in…' the footy club version, not the gospel one we played by mistake.

The atmosphere at funerals varies. The saddest ones are the old singles who have outlived their friends. Empty seats. My Dad had us. I hope I'll still have friends at my send-off. Not just rent-a-crowd.

Weddings are easier because most people want to be there. Like for my sister Bea. She has so many friends who were genuinely pleased she'd found Dan as a partner. I'm learning to match the ceremony to the personalities. Not just the words. But the pace too.

It's a performance.

Previously, I was an actor with too few paid gigs, so I needed regular work. Being a country-based celebrant, my clients often know each other from school ,work or even the footy club.

My job is reading personalities, filling in legal forms and acting as part-time M.C, which can be the Master or Mistress of Ceremonies whichever term you prefer. Anticipating what might go wrong, before it does. Usually I don't stay for the drinks at the wake. Or sit at the wedding breakfast even though the invitation is often given.

As a control-freak, I hate to move from timing everything, to being a guest who is sitting around, waiting.

Unless there is a mystery to solve, then I'm intrigued.

Football Hall of Fame Wedding

Unfortunately the butterflies hadn't thawed.

No wedding photo opportunity!

So they didn't fly around Becky the bride and up into the sky to symbolise re-generation and new life. They stayed in the silver designer-release box, insulated with cooling packs to replicate their natural hibernation. Not sure if butterflies shiver, but these big Monarchs look tightly closed, despite their black, orange and white beauty.

The box is on the terrace. I peer in. Had a few qualms about the speed at which this last-minute wedding was arranged. Not enough time to check on details at the bottom of my to-do list. Especially butterflies.

'Oh no.' Not moving. They weren't really frozen, just chilled. Farm- bred and meant to be released into the wild after fluttering around the bride. Only they weren't.

'Bread-and-butterflies NOT fluttering by', says nervous bridegroom Ollie trying a sort-of- joke. Not the first thing to go wrong for him on this Friday 13th. Finn, his second groomsman hadn't turned up, so the embarrassed second bridesmaid walked solo.

The photographer apologises. 'The butterflies were supposed to be opened earlier, to warm up to local temperature. Some one forgot. We'll organise a refund.'

'Too late for that. We're leaving for our Antarctic expedition tomorrow,' says the disappointed bride. Becky had a desire for tropical coloured romance as part of her hasty wedding before the endless white-out of polar ice. Unfulfilled.

'Sorry darling,' says Ollie. 'I tried.'

'Not your fault,' says Becky who seems a very reasonable girl, especially when last-minute brides are entitled to fuss a bit. 'It's cool.'

They smile at each other. I hope this mutual acceptance lasts, long term. And I also wonder if reject butterflies can be recycled? Currently they're in a box out the back.

These 'cool' butterflies are not really my responsibility as celebrant, but I try to help with romantic extras which include love doves which are not supposed to drop on guests or fly in the wrong direction. Has happened. Helium filled balloons are no longer eco-acceptable and banned in some states.

'The plastic is harmful to sea life,' says the bride. 'I prefer butterflies.'

My choice too, but not for a scientific reason. A box of butterflies is simpler to delegate. One of the groomsmen was supposed to be on today's butterfly duty.

'That was Finn's job.'

But no-one could find Finn.

We didn't know then, that he was dead at the bottom of the back staircase in the Football Hall of Fame. That was NOT scheduled on my running sheet. The small wedding was held in the ultra –modern, see-through foyer of the Hall of Fame. All glass, mirrors and skylights. High heels tapped on the polished wood floor, the footsteps echoing. The bridal party and me as the celebrant were reflected many times, so hopefully a missing groomsman was less obvious to guests who were mainly elderly relatives wearing bi-focal glasses.

'Did you call Finn's mobile?' I ask Joseph the best man

who was sorting extra chairs for guests who didn't want to stand for the short ceremony.

'A few times. No answer. Doesn't mean anything tragic. He's always losing his phone. Or turning it off.'

I request guests to turn off their phones during the ceremony. Part of my new opening routine. If any ringing interrupts, I suggest owners donate to the bride's nominated charity. Hasn't happened but it's an informal start and guests smile at my request, and my admission that I have donated a few times myself to the Salvos, and then they relax.

But I had noticed one left on an empty chair and slip the phone in my pocket, intending to hand it to security, but got side tracked as the ceremony was completed and documents witnessed.

With legalities over, the bride looks happy holding a bouquet of white daisies and fiddling self-consciously with her new wedding band. The groom wears a matching flower in his lapel. About the same height, they kiss, awkwardly.

'Lovely bride.'

'Unusual setting.'

'Love the mirrors.'

Chatting guests gather on the terrace outside amongst the football hero sculptures for the staged photos and butterfly release. Only there isn't one.

'Becky always did have strange ideas,' complains an elderly great-uncle after inspecting the comatose butterflies in their box. 'Where are the drinks? I need a beer.'

After the butterfly non-event, guests move inside to clink glasses and nibble savouries before checking on the seating plan to discover where they are to sit and if they can switch place-names to avoid Great Uncle Peter.

'Why is all the food white?' demands Stella, an activist

cousin who sees racial discrimination everywhere. 'And on white plates?' Her facial jewellery must make eating food of any colour difficult, especially with her jutting lip rings.

'I asked for an Antarctic white theme, Stella,' says Becky. 'Even though 'bergs' have hints of jade green from marine life, especially when they turn over.'

That had been a challenge for SAGE catering. My sister Bea loves even rush-jobs, which are imaginative. Rice rolls with fish. Mini pancakes with cream cheese. Icy sweets. Herb sorbet.

'What's that?' Stella points to a savoury platter and the light reflects on her multiple rings and bracelets. I wonder where else she wears them. Must be a metallic nightmare when she goes through security scanners.

'U.F.O.s. Unidentified food objects,' I suggest.

Guests laugh, enjoying the small wedding doubling up as a farewell party for the couple heading Down South the next day.

'Oh, the tables!' exclaims a delighted guest. 'Like icebergs.'

The white clothed tables are arranged like icebergs on the sea of blue carpet. Penguins, petrels and seals as decoration. Each table is an Antarctic Base with a tiny flag.

'Just a hint of where Becky and Ollie will be for the next year,' explains the best man. 'Working as Dieso and Met-Gnome.'

They were last minute substitutes for the contracted expedition mechanic and meteorologist who'd had to pull out due to a family emergency. Hence the speedy wedding today.

'Love the winterers' job titles. Becky says the blokes are called met-fairies if they are meteorologists,' Joseph, the best man continues. He seems to be trying to cover for the missing groomsman and keep the conversation going. He glances at his fashionable watch.

'Heard your speakers' agency is in trouble, Joseph,' says Stella, the activist cousin with the face jewellery. She must share a few tactless family genes with Ollie. Clumsily, her elbow knocks a champagne glass off the table.

'Who told you that?' the best man turns around so quickly he saves the falling glass without spilling the liquid. For a well padded man, he's light on his feet. Smart mover. Probably a good dancer. He puts the drink back on the table. 'Was it someone here today? Your Great Uncle Peter?'

'Just talk around the sports news blogs. Finn wasn't the only disgraced footballer on a drug charge. Bookings have dropped off.' Joseph owns 'The Best Sport' a speakers' agency representing sports stars. Lucrative agent fees, but not if your star broke contracts, wrecked motel rooms, didn't show up and was becoming notorious rather than a celeb. Or if the rest of the time he was in the headlines for going into rehab – again.

'Is Finn still on your speakers' circuit?'

'No.'

'Did he leave or did you break his contract?'

'That's my business. Confidentiality clause.' Joseph the charming best man turns into his shrewd business self. 'That's why we're called 'The Best Sport'.'

I'm surprised Joseph doesn't seem too concerned that Finn, who is one of his agency clients, is missing. Unless there's been an accident, not turning up to be a groomsman at a wedding is a pretty big insult. So why isn't he worried? Does Joseph know where Finn is? Does he think Finn is safer out of the way? Has Finn been drinking again? Or a repeat of the drug problems that landed him on last night's current affairs SHAME SEGMENT television? And ruined his marketing potential as a brand to sell football gear. Even I had heard of Finn health drinks and Finn running shoes before this wedding.

Trying to change the subject, an older cousin asks Becky, 'Couldn't you have married at the South Pole, Becky?'

'No, we're not going to the South Pole. The Australian base is at Casey Station. That's a long way apart. Look at the ice map.'

Their wedding cake is an ice cream map in the shape of Antarctica, with two albatross to represent the bride and groom. SAGE catering and Bea have excelled.

'Aren't albatross bad luck on ships?' asks the elderly aunt.

'Albatross mate for life,' explains Becky. 'Like us.'

The best man shrugs. 'Best to believe that.'

Friday 13th was not an opportune wedding date for the superstitious. But Becky and Ollie were matter-of-fact types, apart from Becky's butterfly passion.

'No butterflies in Antarctica,' says Great Uncle Peter who had 'bought' the troubled football club and supplied the Hall of Fame free for the hasty reception.

'No butterflies in our wedding photos either,' admits Ollie. 'I'll kill that Finn. Why have a groomsman if he can't get his only job right. I invited him to make him feel included. Lots of ex-fans won't even talk to him. He's been shunned in the last year. In and out of rehab. So, where is he?'

'Forget about Finn. I have. Concentrate on your beautiful bride,' says the best man pouring a chilled champagne. 'I got this bottle from the catering fridge out the back.'

'Thanks.' Ollie toasts his bride. 'To us.'

'Remember. The couple who exercise and work together, stay together,' says the chubby best-man. He'd been divorced twice, Joseph told me earlier when he assured me he was an expert on wedding protocol. I suggest he escort the second bridesmaid on his other arm. He nods.

Why were we in the Football Hall of Fame?

Despite the superstitious refusing to marry on Friday 13th, local function centres were fully booked for conferences, so Great Uncle Peter had 'persuaded' the football club to provide their Hall of Fame for the reception. Trophies, busts and portraits of former players were displayed on the walls. Helpful friends had veiled them with themed white sheets and ribbon decorations so it looked like a series of ghosts watching the guests at the wedding breakfast.

'Fun,' says Becky. 'Like extra guests.'

I like the way she puts a positive spin on events.

'Non-eating guests,' says Great Uncle Peter who is always keen on keeping within budget.

'Did you get your last minute flights to Hobart?'

Becky nods. The superstitious do not fly on the 13th, especially in seats numbered 13 A & B. The 'Polar' re-supply ship was to leave, from Hobart tomorrow and the replacement dieso and meteorologist had to be on it for the change-over voyage. Becky hired her long white dress and veil with daisy patterned lace.

'Only intend using it once, so why spend a fortune.'

But Becky had always longed for a touch of romance and in her mind, butterflies were it. 'Sort of last wild life experience here …before we leave on the Antarctic expedition. No butterflies there.'

'Maybe anxiety about falling down crevasses?' says Ollie the-trying-to-be-reassuring new husband, sipping his champagne.

The bride looks blank.

'That's a different kind of invisible butterflies. In the stomach. We might both have that. Anyway there's seals and penguins ahead of us. More interesting wildlife,' says Ollie who talks himself into more trouble. He's more of a do-er than a talker. Give him any engine and he can fix it.

'Got yellow Caterpillar blood in his veins,' says Great Uncle Peter who appreciates his nephew as a mechanic. Great Uncle Peter owns multiple businesses with Caterpillar vehicles which need servicing, often.

Both Becky and Ollie were outdoor, sporty types with the trim physique of the well exercised. They'd passed the stringent Antarctic medical and done search & rescue training earlier. Been kitted out in cold weather gear by the Antarctic Division. Living and working in an isolated community for a year was not your average honeymoon. Especially when most of the expeditioners were males with an overdose of the adventure gene.

'Lucky you got the Notice of Intended Marriage form in within the one month's notice.'

'Didn't want to lose Becky,' says Ollie. An astute celebrant picks up a lot in the pre-wedding briefings. Quick emotional histories. Like job interviews for life. This couple were physically adventurous but emotionally vulnerable. Often it's what they don't say.

Few females work on Antarctic expeditions. The ratio was definitely in favour of females choosing the male partner. Ollie was nervous about losing his very attractive fiancée. So he wanted to marry, now.

'Couldn't you get married on the ship? Doesn't the captain do stuff like that?' asks an elderly aunt.

'The station leader on the base has legal powers, but…'

Ollie couldn't believe that a girl like Becky had accepted his proposal.

'Any girl is a 10 in Antarctica, even my Becky.'

'You mean Becky is not very attractive?' says Great Uncle Peter in his 'not–wearing-my-hearing-aids-voice.

Becky looks up.

Ollie blushes. 'No…what I meant was…Hey, has anyone seen Finn?'

'His portrait is still in the foyer. I told security to take it down.' Great Uncle Peter had been a keen footballer in his youth. 'Finn shouldn't be there. Not after all that drugs business. And Finn's name on the champions' trophy on the first floor landing. That has to go. He should be wiped out of club history.'

I had met Finn at the wedding rehearsal.

The ex-footballer had shoulders which strained the seams of his rarely used navy suit. His thighs were like solid tree trunks. His hair was shaven to an almost bald cut, pretending to be fashionable but from the back view his half moon circled scalp showed middle-aged hair in decline. I prefer a male to be honestly bald at any age. Not an issue yet for my partner Art. He still has his curly dark hair. But knees and ankles are a problem for most experienced athletes. Finn moved as if he had joint problems, in both legs and his neck.

Finn's final footy performance had been at a highly televised match when he made a crucial goal but unfortunately in the wrong direction. End of game. End of premiership and end of his career. No more sponsors. Couldn't even get a country coaching job after that. Known as the man who faced the wrong way.

I was surprised kindly Ollie invited him to be part of the wedding party. But they went to primary school together.

Meanwhile the guests have finished the nibbles and sorted their seating.

Great Uncle Peter ignored his recycled place-name and sat next to the second bridesmaid who tried to escape to the Ladies. 'I'll just freshen up before the speeches,' she suggests.

The ground floor Ladies was being used so the bridesmaid goes upstairs.

She gets lost on her way back.

A loud scream. Everybody runs to help. The bridesmaid is quivering.

'The butterflies are out!'

'They thawed!'

The big Monarch butterflies are flitting all over the room and stairs. Colourful but also a little menacing as they flutter inside, darting around people's heads and on shoulders. One is on the bridesmaid's arm. She shakes it away. And then they hover, quivering around the dark mound lying on the floor.

The bridesmaid lets out another scream. And points.

'There's a body at the bottom of the back stairs!'

'It's Finn.'

'Has he collapsed?'

'Is he drunk?'

'He seems to have been attacked.'

Hard to miss that very solid football trophy fallen sideways on the step. A significant weapon. Someone had used it to flatten Finn's skull. And then he'd fallen or was pushed down the back staircase. Blood stains marked his fall. Such a big man but motionless now sprawled across the bottom step. All those years of muscle training wasted.

'He's been killed?' The bridesmaid can't believe it. 'Finn was supposed to be my partner for the wedding. And he didn't turn up!'

Guests mill around unsure what to do. They flap their arms to shoo away the butterflies which suddenly seem menacing rather than beautiful. The insects congregate towards the high, glass, fake sky of the skylights, flapping aimlessly until someone opens the lower doors and most flee. You don't expect death at a wedding. Nor to be mobbed by flapping, silent insects, touching on your face and arms, intruding on your skin, unless you keep moving. Finn's body is not moving. I shoo the butterflies away from the blood on his head and shoulders. I try not to think of why they are attracted there.

The guests fall silent, watching me. Only a few clattering noises from catering staff returning trays in the kitchen remind of the daily routine of the real world. I'm the MC, but a murder scene is not on my to-do list. Despite this, I simultaneously calculate the angle of Finn's fall as I ring the police and shepherd the shocked guests back into the reception area. More likely a push than a fall. Security arrives but he's a uniformed ditherer more used to lost property duty. That's when I remember the lost phone in my other pocket.

I take it out.

'That's Finn's phone,' says Cousin Stella as she ushers the bridesmaid away. 'I recognise the cover.'

It was unlocked. No password.

You must decide today. This was the last text message. Dated and timed.

The Football Hall of Fame had back and front stairs access. The modern entrance was often used for sporting media events, and the foyer had flattering lighting suitable for television interviews. But the back stairs were mainly used by staff carrying trays of food and drink. Bea told me that her catering staff preferred the service lift.

'Had he been drinking?' asks a guest flicking away a stray butterfly.

Finn doesn't smell of alcohol. I checked.

'No. He doesn't drink any more. Or so he says…er…said. Not since the police charged him after he crashed the car,' Ollie explains. Difficult to get used to past tense when a big personality is no longer present.

'Drugs?'

'The start of his problems…' says Ollie with his arm around the shaking Becky

'Football fans are so one- eyed. Like religious fanatics. But not enough to kill him, surely? '

Becky shakes her head. She's in shock.

Finn's body was in front of her. Blood red on the carpeted stairs. This was reality not romance.

It also meant a murderer amongst the guests or the catering staff.

At that realisation, Becky lost it!

'AAAhhh…' She collapses sobbing. Ollie tries to calm her.

'At OUR WEDDING? Who would do such a terrible, terrible thing?'

Back in the hall, the ice cream wedding cake is melting. Staff put it temporarily in the freezer.

Icebergs are 9/10s under the surface.

Like motives. Who did it? Who murdered the groomsman with the football trophy on the wedding day?

You must decide today.

What was it that Finn had to decide today? To leave the football world? To keep quiet? To sign a contract? Or NOT to do something?

I knew who had sent the message. But not why.

Finn was now beyond making his own decisions. Sad

that shock rather than loss was the common reaction of the wedding guests to his violent death. At the crime-scene, no-one had cried at losing him. I'd hate to be in that situation. But you wouldn't know if you were dead and alone.

Maybe if I found out the truth, it would be a kind of resolution for him? The real victims were the bride and groom and their wedding day memories. Finn was a local footy tragedy: a man so good at his chosen sport that he destroyed himself. Just because a man could kick a ball well, and that skill was obscenely paid, didn't make him a hero. That was the flaw. Ego. Believing your own publicity. Quite Shakespearean really. Sad.

After the police left, taking Finn's phone as evidence and the body of Finn was taken away by the coroner's staff, I was left with the shaken guests at the destroyed wedding breakfast. All the butterflies had fled except one stray perched on the highest of the shrouded statues. We left it there. I'll never feel the same way about butterflies again. No-one felt like eating. Not even the melting cake which hadn't actually been cut.

'Should we cut the cake?'

'Doesn't seem appropriate.'

So staff put it back in the freezer a second time.

The police gave permission for Ollie and Becky to catch their 7 pm plane. Some honeymoon! But they were cleared as murder suspects. They had been witnessed all morning getting ready so neither could have attacked Finn.

'I'm so sorry I said I'd kill him, when he didn't do the butterflies,' admits Ollie. 'But it's just one of those phrases. I didn't mean it.'

Becky was distraught. 'And then Great Uncle Peter refused to invest.'

'Invest in what? He already owns the football club,' Stella is intrigued by unfolding events.

'Buy a majority share in 'The Best Sport'.' Becky's eyes are red with crying, despite the bridesmaid's best attempts at patching makeup.

'Why would he?' asks Stella. 'The agency is failing according to my contacts.'

'So it would promote Great Uncle Peter's club players, instead of Finn's failed brand,' says Becky.

'Unlikely,' says Ollie. 'Great Uncle Peter is savvy about his money. Earned it the hard way.'

Stella knows her elderly relative too. 'He's a long term planner. Makes strategic alliances. Never makes bad investments.' The light glints on her face jewellery and I wonder if she'll ever consider that a bad investment. Maybe face jewellery is a disguise for a keen brain? A distraction?

Meanwhile, I'm having suspicions about Joseph. He had my running sheet. He knows the procedures for weddings. So he knew where everybody would be at a certain time. And that message on Finn's phone had come from The Best Sport agency.

You must decide today.

Maybe Joseph was the best man for the murder suspect?

I need a quiet chat with Cousin Stella about him.

In her other life, Stella is a small time blogger with aspirations to big time media, who likes to be seen as an expert on politics, sport and anything 'activist' which just about covers everything.

'I wondered when you might ask me for the inside story, Quinn,' says Stella. She gives me her version of the facts.

Joseph was heading for financial ruin, according to Stella. Finn was a liability not an asset. Sponsors didn't want to work with any sportsperson from the same agency as the disgraced Finn. And the BIG money of Finn's name on merchandise? Wasn't happening anymore. Every time Finn opened his mouth, like on last night's TV program, and talked about his involvement with sports drugs, The Best Sport value went down.

'Thanks Stella.' If she puts any of those observations on her blog, she'll have big-time legal issues. But she probably knows that already. She's had a few issues with 'borrowing' research done by others, according to Art.

Meanwhile, sitting at the defunct bridal table, surrounded by the white draped ghosts of past players, Great Uncle Peter holds court.

'Finn ruined the name of my club. I invested a lot of my hard earned cash in rescuing this footy club. I was never good enough to play in a grand final. But I let others have their chance. I paid for their opportunities. Then Finn mocks me. Says the club is a has-been and so am I.'

I ask. 'Were you near the back stairs with Finn? On the first floor?'

Great Uncle Peter looks astonished. 'Me? Can't get up the stairs. Heart problems. And I can barely reach his shoulder.'

'But you argued with him?' I query, remembering the goods service lift with first floor access.

'I told him what I thought. That's not an argument. Ruined the only chance our club had of a premiership. So I told him that. I couldn't hear his answer too well, my hearing aid you know, so I grabbed his arm. That's when the trophy fell off the stand.'

'So you were on the first floor landing near the stairs? That's where the trophy was, on the stand. Did you use the goods service lift to get to the first floor?'

Great Uncle Peter looks directly at me.

'Of course. Old men like me need to get to the Gents quickly. The toilets below were being used.'

I'm reminded he owns this club, so he'd know all the exits.

'Was Finn still alive when you finished arguing…er telling him and the trophy fell over?'

'Yes. That trophy is very heavy. I left it for Finn or someone else to pick up.'

'Was Finn still alive when you left to come down in the lift.'

'With my legs, going down stairs is harder than going up. Of course I got the lift down.'

It's only later that I realise Great Uncle Peter didn't answer my questions. He deflected them. He didn't lie about things for which he might later be accountable. A wily operator.

I turn to Joseph. 'Did you notice anything around the back stairs when you went out back for the champagne in the catering fridge?'

'Tell Quinn what was really going on,' commands Great Uncle Peter.

Joseph seems to be making a decision. You could see it in his face. As if he'd given up. Was cutting his losses. (Only later I realised what an excellent actor Joseph was. As a part-time actor myself, I appreciate Joseph's skills but not his motives.)

'Finn had become a liability. He couldn't keep his mouth shut. And he was dragging the reputation of my other speakers and the agency down with him.'

'So…' encourages Great Uncle Peter.

'They kept the football trophy on display on the first floor. I was looking at his engraved name when he came up behind me, talking on his phone. He taunted me that he had been added to the Hall of Fame. He didn't deserve that. So I told him,' says Joseph.

'Were you involved in his death on Becky and Ollie's WEDDING DAY?'

Joseph ignores the direct question. Perhaps he feared I was recording him. (I was.) And there were possible witnesses amongst the listening guests.

'I'd gone out back to check on the champagne supplies. Heard him talking on his mobile to Sports News. Offering an exclusive for a big fee. It would totally destroy my Agency's reputation. Especially as Great Uncle Peter had just told me he refused to invest in The Best Sport to keep us afloat.'

Great Uncle Peter nods. 'That's true.'

'I challenged him for the mobile phone. I wanted to speak to Sports News. We wrestled. Even though Finn was out of condition by his standards, he was 90% fitter than me. He threw the phone down the stairs, I went after it. When I turned, he was out of sight and I thought he'd left…must have slipped against the trophy and hit his head open…'

I didn't believe a word of that. And Joseph's defence lawyers would have a difficult time proving his innocence.

'What time was this? Was it before or after the butterflies NOT flying at 2.40?'

'Before of course. Finn wasn't in the wedding procession.'

'True. But he also wasn't there to unthaw the butterflies at 1.45. So was he dead then? Most people would go back up the stairs and help him. Why didn't you?'

Joseph stood thinking for a response that would clear him. The text message on the phone was the problem for him. And it was in police hands. Plus I'd picked up Finn's phone from the foyer chair BEFORE the 2pm wedding and Joseph was claiming he saw Finn talking on that phone earlier. He was the last one to do so. And he had a financial motive for wanting to remove Finn, permanently.

'Hypothetically, if I'd killed Finn before the wedding, why would I go near the stairs later to get the champagne for Ollie to toast the bride? Surely I'd stay away so someone else would find him?'

Joseph had sweat on his plump forehead now.

Great Uncle Peter interrupts. 'I'd already told Joseph at 1.30. I wasn't putting money into his business to save it. I'm his alibi. At 1.25 when I saw Finn, he was alive. So Joseph had no reason to kill him. The Best Sport was finished.'

'Hypothetically, maybe Joseph was just checking as no-one had noticed Finn's death yet. And he wanted to know why?'

How did Finn's mobile get onto the spare seat in the foyer?

If Joseph put it there, why didn't he just wipe the messages?

Did he get side tracked when asked to fill in as the extra bridesmaid escort?

While these questions were racing around my head, the bridesmaid makes an announcement into the microphone.

'The bride and groom are now leaving on their honeymoon. Let's give them a farewell cheer.'

The remaining guests re-group on the terrace and wave to the subdued bridal couple.

They don't throw the confetti. Or rice, which is ecologically more acceptable.

The 'Just Married' sign attached to the car earlier seems out-of-place, with the dangling horseshoe for good luck, but the bridesmaid catches the daisy bouquet Becky throws.

'You'll be next,' Great Uncle Peter says.

'To marry or to be murdered?' comments Cousin Stella. She turns to me.

'Skype me tomorrow Quinn. I'll have something to share with you by then.'

You must decide today

That night I tossed, getting twisted up in the sheets which became part of my dreams. I was like the shrouded footy statues. Bound. Couldn't see. I fought to get free. But in my dream, my sheets had turned into lists of things I hadn't done. Inky notes. On white sheets. Notes I couldn't read. Upside down. Illegible. Confining me. Then I woke up, sweaty, with a residual fear. I knew I'd missed something. Sheets! I got up, the perspiration drying on me, and checked my running sheet for the wedding. Then I drew the floor plan for all floors of the Football Hall of Fame, including the stairs and service lifts. There were two. I'd missed the second goods lift earlier.

You must decide today

I jot down a murder timetable. Who was where and when? I drew little coloured figures and dots for their tracks.

Then the answer dawned.

My mistake was I'd been looking for one killer. Not two.

And maybe that text message was intended for more than one person.

Joseph sent Finn a text, *You must decide today* about NOT speaking on sports media in an expose. But maybe Joseph had also sent that to Great Uncle Peter, deliberately, to save time, and for a decision on investing.

Maybe they were in it together, conspiring to get rid of Finn and be alibis for each other?

If Great Uncle Peter and Joseph worked together on removing Finn. THEN Great Uncle Peter would invest at a rate highly advantageous to him. Few other options for Joseph who was physically able, but Great Uncle Peter was the strategist.

At 6 am Stella Skypes me. 'You look like shit Quinn. Couldn't you sleep either?' Her face appears on my screen. I'm getting used to the face jewellery. I don't think she killed Finn. No motive or opportunity. So I'm prepared to listen to her ideas. Even if some of her research methods are questionable.

'Could it have been two people?' Stella suggests.

'Yes. Working together.' I say.

'That's a relief. Thought I was going mad. But I know more of our weirdo family background than you.' Stella's jewellery glints as she speaks seriously. 'Great Uncle Peter was involved in dodgy dealings early on. Often his competitors were 'removed'. Womaniser. Predator. We learnt to keep out of his way as young girls. Offered the hall of fame as a free wedding venue. Maybe so he could control events? Unfortunate to have a death during the wedding, but thought they had more chance of getting away with it…and the timing was crucial. If Finn was pouring out his guts with a TV expose…'

'He'd already gone public on the T.V. current affair the night before.'

'That just escalated the urgency of getting rid of him.'

Intriguing how Cousin Stella's vocabulary changes. She fluctuates between footy talk, reportage and psychology babble. She plays different roles too. I check my diagram with my arrows and times. And my notes.

'Sounds possible to me. What about Joseph?'

'Sending you an attachment. With the times. Who did what. I've put a question mark where I'm not sure.'

'OK. Just don't put it on your blog by mistake.'

Instantly the attachment arrives. Digital detection at its best!

But Cousin Stella's checklist overdosed on question marks.

And words. Bloggers need lots of personal details. Must be a payment per word habit.

1.25 G-U Peter argues w Finn @ top of stairs re name on trophy.

1.30 G-U refused to invest.

Joseph overhears Finn accepting expose offer he told him to reject???

Argue. Finn throws phone down stairs???

Joseph takes phone into foyer. Sits. Phone falls out of his pocket???

1.50 Finn NOT available to thaw butterflies.

Joseph distracted by having to double up with bridesmaids. Finn a no-show.

2.00 -2.30 Ceremony.

2.40 Butterfly release planned.

2.50 Joseph goes behind scenes to get champagne but Finn already dead…(ALIBI?)

I look up at Stella's concerned face waiting on my screen and the light glints on the ring jutting from her lip. My notes are shorter but we've come to the same conclusion.

They are her relatives which makes it more difficult for Stella. But Ollie and Becky are my clients. I already feel that I've let them down with things going so wrong around the ceremony.

'I agree with you Stella. Finn was already dead, otherwise he would have appeared earlier in the bridal group. Joseph was getting the champagne as his alibi.'

Stella lets out a sigh. 'Now we'll have to deal with the fallout from Great Uncle Peter's businesses. Ollie won't have a job to come back to.'

'Mmm. Won't his Antarctic experience help?'

Stella shrugs. 'Maybe.'

Murdering businessmen create work, but the wrong kind.

We share our theories with the police who reach the same conclusion about our suspects. They arrest both. But Great Uncle Peter's lawyer gets busy immediately and they are released on a bond. The legal delaying tactics start.

I wish I'd offered Becky and Ollie the elopement package which is just the basic, legal ceremony. They could have avoided the heartache of unthawed butterflies and the murder of their groomsman. And Friday 13th angst. Could have performed the legal stuff in a park en route for the airport as I did for a couple once before. Should have done that for Becky & Ollie. En route for Antarctica.

Cousin Stella emails me her Football Tragic
Football is just a game, a poor player
who mouths and kicks his hour upon the ground
And then is heard no more. It is a fake-religion,
A brand, bought by a fan, full of sound and fury,
Signifying nothing.
I'm not sure how to respond.

Committed!

He is choking. It is SO fast. Like botched cosmetic surgery, his lips swell. His eyes water. He is gasping for breath.

Max drops the plate of fried rice and the grains scatter across the ruby red carpet, like discarded confetti.

He grabs his throat and drops to the floor, one foot twitching in the lime -green sneaker with the black laces. Long, skinny legs. Fat ankles in unmatching striped socks. Strange how my mind registers details like this in the midst of an emergency. As if he's got dressed in a hurry. Or is posing as arty. Or trying to fit his personalized Rock -Legend interpretation of this Seventies party theme?

He groans and then gasps VERY loudly. Sandy and Alex, the guests- of- honour who have been dancing nearby, turn around at the noise and hurry towards him. I am further away, up on the platform, adjusting the microphone, which is still on and sensitive enough to pick up Max's disturbing noises and amplify them with an electronic screech throughout the hall.

'EEEEEHHHH'

The area below is packed with forty-something dancing friends of the popular forty-something couple who had just committed to their relationship in public. I flick off the microphone. From the platform, I can see him collapsing.

'Not Max, again!' Sandy rushes over. 'Use the Epi-pen.'

'Is it that 'Ana….whatever…reaction to nuts?' cries Alex anxiously following her new wife.

Max is trying to vomit.

Embarrassed guests react at his ugly gasps, the mess of vomit and the noise of his fork and spoon hitting the plate as they fall from his hands.

'Give him Epinephrine. Inject it in his thigh,' says Sandy.

'Where is the injection?' I'm not sure if I can cope with injecting him, but I'll try. The others seemed stunned and want to distance themselves from him.

'Check his pockets.'

One of the guests goes through Max's pockets to find the Epi-pen.

'Not there. No medication either.'

'Anyone got one?' a resourceful guest loosens Max's collar. Stunned guests shake their heads as Max keeps gasping.

So I call the ambulance. This emergency is such an unfair way for Sandy and Alex to start a new life together after bankruptcy, cancer and losing their gallery. Today is meant to be a celebration of their commitment to each other. And until now, I've been emcee of a fun event with great dance music, despite the temperamental microphone.

Cassandra, his ex-mother-in-law watches dispassionately from a side chair. Not sure how much she understands of anything. She shares a variation of her name with her daughter, but not much else.

'Off with the pixies,' quickly excuses Alex as she follows my glance. 'But occasionally she's lucid. Parts of the brain work still but you never know when that will be. Loves me as a new daughter-in-law but can't remember why. And hates Max.'

The para-medics arrive very quickly, festooned with digital medical gadgets. So many attachments dangling from their belts. Their navy uniformed, fit bodies are reassuringly official as they bring hope and the necessary life-lines.

But it is too late.

Now Max is quiet and his body lies on the carpet. Respectful and efficient team- work moves him onto the stretcher which is flat on the ruby carpet.

'One, two. Lift'

I notice the female para-medic is equal height with her male colleague and wonder if the staffing schedules match them on height so it's easier to lift stretchers.

Not like plumbers who need to be small to fix messy jobs and crawl through small pipes under buildings. Plumbers! Height requirements! My mind is wandering around trivia to avoid thinking about the implications of this death. Not the kind of memory you want from your special day if you are the couple. As the celebrant, I want to solve their problems, but a stalking ex husband who has a fatal allergic attack is not fixable.

I glance at the other guests. They looked stunned too, especially the man in the tan trousers with the very wide bottoms and a woeful fashion sense in any decade. Flares that badly cut weren't even on trend in the Seventies.

'Can't believe this is happening,' he says. 'Not to Max.'

But it has. He's been told to 'piss off' by many people, according to his ex-wife, but this was an accident. Or was it?

'Ready?' says the male para- medic. 'I've already called the coroner's staff.'

A rattle and squeak of the stretcher, as the para-medics adjust the height up to hip level, flick the brake off and wheel him to the ambulance. The brilliantly lit back of the ambulance looks like a mini operating theatre with monitoring equipment. But it is no longer needed. They have to wait for the forensic pathologist and the coroner's staff to remove the body.

The Coroner's vehicle arrives.

'He's had a bad reaction,' they murmur to Sandy when she explains she is his ex-wife. 'Anaphylaxis is an allergic reaction. Not usually this severe.'

Sandy has mixed emotions on her face. Hard to read. Loss, regret and maybe guilt? She's still wearing her short ABBA outfit, with a blonde wig, their choice instead of bridal gowns for the ceremony.

Max was the ex-husband who did not approve of this same -sex relationship. He'd been very vocal running an anti-lesbian campaign in public. Sandy and Alex had not expected him to attend the party.

'After they split, he often stalked Sandy,' Alex explains. 'And he ruined her business with a smear campaign.'

He hadn't been invited. But he had appeared at the venue, argued with Sandy and so Bea had offered a drink and food to calm him down.

The police are called. As the guests are interviewed, the retro Seventies costumes look garish and out- of -place. Lots of blonde wigs. Multiple ABBAs, rock singers, short skirts, lemon -yellow and pink. Fake Rock -legends. Flares. And one lime green sneaker with black laces left behind, which Alex picks up.

Bea is distraught. She pulls me aside. 'If my catering killed him, that's the end of my SAGE business! But I didn't have any nuts in there. I had labels on ALL the food. Always do. Did you know if he was allergic to seafood or berries? Could it have been that in the fried rice?'

I try to quieten my sister. 'Calm down Bea. I'll find out. His reaction might not have had anything to do with your food.'

Such a colourful buffet. Chicken in apricot sauce.

Caramelised orange slices. Beef Wellington encased in pastry. Seafood cocktails. Bea has themed the Seventies food based on the popular cook book of that period. Notice lots of the grilled grapefruit left. Accurate for the period but unpopular then and now?

'But guests will THINK it had something to do with MY food' says Bea. 'Oh that sounds heartless. Sorry. But reputation matters around here. And I took ages to get those Angels on Horseback right.' She points to the bacon wrapped prunes.

Guests come up to Sandy to give her hugs and sympathy. 'Our condolences Sandy.'

Sandy seems outwardly calmer now. She is rationalizing, 'I've been avoiding Max for months. Even took out an intervention order against him for stalking. Me accepting condolences doesn't seem right.'

'You were the closest to him. It helps others to say the usual condolences even if they didn't like him,' says Alex putting an arm around her. 'They don't know what else to say or do.'

That's true. As the celebrant of an unexpectedly interrupted ceremony, for once I had no advice. I knew of a funeral where an elderly relative had passed away peacefully in the last minutes of the ceremony. But that had been a quiet slumping, and funeral parlour staff had discreetly looked after him once the others had left the chapel. This was different.

'Should I have gone with Max in the ambulance? No-one should die alone,' says Sandy.

'Too late now,' soothes Alex. 'And we were all here.'

The room is crowded with friends of the popular Sandy BUT… none were Max's friends. He was a man with no mates.

They'd put up with him when he was part of the Sandy-Max couple, but once Alex came on the scene, they dumped Max.

These were the friends of Sandy and later of Alex as they became the recognised couple.

Sandy and Alex seem well suited, except for the emotional baggage of a stalking ex-husband and a mother with waves of dementia.

'Sandy, do you mind me asking which foods Max was allergic to?' I ask.

Sandy shrugs.

'Usually he avoided seafood. I knew about peanuts and other nuts but I didn't know about barberries. Is that what caused it?'

'Not sure.'

Sandy glances towards the corner seat where her mother is sitting, staring blankly.

Cassandra had been quiet in the corner, during the dancing and while the para-medics had attended to Max.

She wore the same unassuming navy outfit she'd worn in the real Seventies and had worn every decade since. But she ate eagerly from every plate Bea passed around, recognizing food she used to cook.

'My mother suggested including the fried rice with barberries. And we were trying to include her in the ceremony, so I passed on the suggestion to Bea.'

'Had Max choked on specific food before? Any warning signs?'

'Usually the lips swell. Or the throat is itchy. Sometimes he vomits. But the main symptom is not being able to breathe.'

Sandy sounds quite matter-of-fact.

'How often has it happened to Max?'

'A few times. We were at my mother's place a year ago. I

thought he was going to die then, not now.' Someone passes Sandy a tissue but she's not crying, just shocked by the speed of events.

'Didn't he have to carry a pen or something?' asks Alex. 'Typical of Max not to have it.'

Another interruption! Cassandra stands up and booms.

'Max was never good about following instructions.'

Everybody turns in surprise when his ex-mother-in-law interrupts. Cassandra's voice is so loud it is as though she has just been switched on maximum volume. Usually she just sits there, on remote.

'Max wouldn't learn how to use chopsticks.' Cassandra adds loudly.' Everyone should know how to use chopsticks and Epi-pens.'

Automatically tidying in housewifely mode, she picks up the spoon and fork with the plate, but then the police indicate they will need to bag those.

Her friends were told Sandy's mother is getting very vague and forgetting things. But she sounds very 'on the ball 'to me and at the rehearsal she knew what was going on. In between the bouts of silence, her voice is very definite and loud. She has strong opinions but sometimes they get misfiled in the emotional compartments of her memory.

Alex tries to lead her back to the chair, but Cassandra pushes her away angrily.

'All Max's family get asthma. And he had trouble with pollen and breathing each Spring. And Max was on blood pressure tablets too,' says daughter Sandy as she watches her mother tidying aimlessly now. 'He knew some foods put him at risk. We knew too.'

Barberries in the fried rice. Those little purple-black delicacies that Bea had included for the party menu after

Sandy and Alex suggested them even though they weren't around in the Seventies. Meant to be healthy. Were they the cause?

I check Dr Google quickly. If I can find out online, so can others.

'Barberry may interfere with some medications including antihistamines, blood thinners and blood pressure medication.'

Sounds like Max used most of those medications. And who knew that? Cassandra?

'Max ruined my daughter's life. And now he's gone,' Cassandra pronounces and sits down of her own accord.

That was not a confession, just a LOUD statement.

And now she talks again in booming bursts of candour. Can't shut her up. Alex tries again and fails. Cassandra pushes her away roughly.

'My daughter deserves happiness. Max never worked. He ruined her gallery. Alex is an artist. She will help with the new gallery.'

Cassandra doesn't seem to connect the Alex she pushes away with the new daughter-in-law she likes. Bits of the brain are not connecting?

Confusing when parents give their children variations of their own name. Ego or fond legacy? What else was Cassandra trying to control? Her ex-son-in-law?

Sandy apologises. 'Just ignore that. My mother isn't really responsible. She forgets things. Her mind has been going. Or Cassandra gets a fixation on some idea but can't remember why.'

Cassandra sits down and goes quiet again, in her own thoughts. Back on remote.

The police have taken away the fried rice container, and

samples from the other food. No-one feels like eating anyway. I wasn't sure how to continue with the change in mood, but luckily I'd already done the ceremony. It would be crass to keep the lively music playing so I turned it off.

Bea grabs my arm. 'Max said to me that he had come to the party because Sandy had sent him an invitation. That's what they were arguing about earlier and I offered him a drink, to distract him.'

'If Sandy didn't send him the invitation, who did?'

'Sandy's mother. She likes Alex. And she never liked Max who suggested Sandy's cancer scare was faked. Her mother thought the worry about Max caused Sandy's breast cancer, whatever the doctors said.'

Revenge? In her on-off mind, Cassandra might have linked barberries with allergies and getting rid of a hated ex son-in law. But that would have been difficult to do… or prove.

I thought about what happened earlier and wondered what I had missed.

Sandy and Alex had booked me as celebrant for their 'party'. SAGE café was catering and has a reputation for tasty and original food, often 'on theme'.

'Nostalgic food of the Seventies,' was ordered by Alex and Sandy.

'Margaret Fulton style?' suggests Bea who collects vintage cookbooks. 'That was the recipe Bible of the period.'

'We don't want a wedding look-alike, more of a party with friends. Music. Good food. A bit of dancing. And just slip the commitment words into the middle. Is that okay?'

'Do you want to write your own words?' I ask.

'Can you write them Quinn? We've heard you've got a bit of a reputation.'

'OK.' I didn't ask what for.

'Don't want to dress as brides. So we're having a Retro-Seventies theme.'

'Up to you.'

'I don't feel comfortable having a gift register. Seems greedy. Sandy and I have enough pots and pans. We already have two of most things,' says Alex.

'I'll suggest a donation to a charity if anyone asks. Which charity do you prefer?'

'Domestic Violence,' Sandy and Alex say it together. Then smile wryly.

Weird how these organisations use the name of the problem they are trying to combat. It's the Bullying Lobby, not the anti-bullying. Or Domestic Violence, not anti-domestic violence.

Maybe ease of online searching?

I make notes. So far they've mentioned what they don't want. Not what they do. 'How do you want the hall set up?'

'Don't want the chairs in rows like a church. Need dance space.'

On the couple's instructions, I left the chairs casually arranged.

But the moment I called for attention from the microphone, guests started arranging their folding chairs in little rows all facing one direction— in front of an invisible 'altar'.

'Let's just sit in a circle,' suggests Alex. Alex seems to be the better organizer. So their next Gallery business might have more hope of success.

'Been living in the flat together for a couple of years, but we knew each other earlier when we worked together. Even before Max and Sandy married.'

'That was a BIG mistake,' says Cassandra, Sandy's mother.

'Marriage or Max?'

'Both. Alex has always been single. Sensible girl,' decreed Cassandra and then tuned out into her remote state.

The couple are adamant about ex-husband Max not being invited.

ə♥

But Max did come to the party and then he went.

So whose fault was that?

We're siblings but Bea doesn't look like me. I'm just mousey brown. Her hair colour changes more often. She's a shorthaired blonde with streaks now. Used to be a longhaired brunette. With all her kitchen work, cramming short hair under a chef's hat is easier. We're similar in our attitudes to clients. We feel responsible. Too much sometimes. She's totally responsible for researching menus and the quality of her food, which is usually fabulous. And any suggestion of poisoning guests will kill her business.

'We don't know the barberries were the problem. That was just a possibility,' I reassure. 'Perfectly healthy food normally.'

'What if there had been other guests with an adverse reaction to barberries?'

'No one else is throwing up, Bea.' I wave at the groups of guests earnestly hanging out together to share the tragedy and trying to understand it.

'But none of the other guests were on Max's combination of medications. And Cassandra knew that.' Bea's frown lines are deepening.

'Maybe it's just all in her muddled head? Very drastic to

kill your ex-son-in-law so your daughter can have a fresh start. And get away from a stalker.' I was talking to my little sister. Not the sort of thing I would share with a client.

'No guarantee he'd have an allergic reaction. He mightn't even eat the fried rice.'

'But I gave him a plateful.' wails Bea.

'Did Cassandra want to stop the ceremony?'

'No. Well I don't think so. She liked Alex. Called her daughter-in-law rather than Sandy's partner.'

Often difficult to know what to call partners. Life-partner sounds pretentious. Business partner is work only. I call Art 'my partner' and leave it up to others to work out our relationship. We've never had a ceremony. Too much like homework for me.

Bea grabs my arm.

'You know Cassandra used to work in computers. She helped me research the Margaret Fulton recipes. She's quite computer savvy…in-between. You just have to get her on a good day or a good few minutes. Must be a different part of the brain which still works on automatic.'

'Maybe.' I have my doubts about Cassandra.

'Cassandra told me she'd had been at a Seniors' afternoon tea last year when one of the guests had an anaphylactic shock after eating barberries. She checked online then.'

I shake my head. 'Too many variables.'

I have my suspicions. But no proof. Cassandra knew Max had attacks before.

She was computer savvy. She might have checked online. AND Max had stalked her daughter.

Can't think of any reason I could prove

Cassandra is not exactly a reliable narrator.

But then, maybe I am not either.

Luckily for Bea, there was no link between her catering and Max's death. The police forensics reassured her.

Cassandra interrupts LOUDLY. 'I like Margaret Fulton's apricot chicken best. When I checked online about the barberries, I found a photo just like the chicken I used to make when you were young Sandy. Remember?'

Sandy stares at her mother. It's as if she's suddenly seeing a familiar face as a stranger. This person used to be her mother. Wrinkles. Thinning hair. Pale skin. But now maybe Cassandra has killed someone? The hazel eyes are dull. Something is missing behind them. Is the memory just selecting what she wants to remember and deliberately losing other acts in the dementia filing cabinet of the mind?

Can her mother be a killer? Which genes might be passed on?

Alex puts her arm around her partner. They hug. Some things cannot be said.

I have my suspicions too. Best to err on the side of compassion. And fix what you can in the present.

With Sandy's permission, I transfer the Domestic Violence donations to the society but label them Anti-Domestic Violence.

'Maybe in memory of Max?' I suggest.

They nod.

All ceremonies have challenges. Couples with different religious views. Complicated domestic arrangements, they want to acknowledge in public. Even multi-parent stepfamilies acknowledging inter relationships of new twigs and branches in their family tree. Almost a family forest!

But I have a gift for the couple. A beautiful piece of artwork, a framed poster signed by their guests in memory of their commitment. It's an updated version of the Jewish custom of ketubah. Cross cultural customs often soothe.

Maybe Sandy and Alex can display it in their new Gallery?

Next day I refuse a commitment ceremony request where the bride is madly in love and so is the groom, but she's a single mum and wants to retain her government benefits. They want to pretend it's a real marriage for the relatives, but not do the legal stuff. I refuse. I don't do fake weddings. And it's illegal.

I also refuse to do SHAM wedding ceremonies for celebrities who are already secretly married but want the exposure for their fading careers and intend selling the exclusive story to the magazines at a sum larger than the cost of catering for 300 guests at The Mansion in our regional town. Not legal. And even though having a celebrant fee ten times the usual offered, it's not ethical. So I said no to that one too.

One Wedding and a Funeral

'Will you join the bridal photo please Quinn?'

'Coming.'

Ours is a small country town and everybody knows at least one member of your family or went to school with them. 'The Village' as locals call Everest Residential Community, is a significant employer of locals. Including me. Their versatile chapel venue can be styled for funerals or weddings, but I work other places too. Like beach weddings. Or rotundas in parks, just in case it rains. Gourmet function centres like The Mansion, who recently put up their prices, are significantly more expensive for the family which may increase the money tensions, but I do a few of those fashionable gigs too.

'Your fees are so reasonable,' said the corporate couple.

They mean I'm cheap, by their standards. I prefer to give extra value.

And why I never charge for solving mysteries.

Satisfaction is important. But happiness ever-after isn't guaranteed.

I have my personal formula. Quinn's Theory of Relativity. The likelihood of the relationship ending in divorce is directly related to the number of arguments during rehearsals, obsessive preparation and the bride's budget on self. Unfortunately for Flora's ceremony, I forgot to factor in the toxic family.

But others are a joy to share. Did a memorable wedding in a hot air balloon with only a witness, bride, groom and the pilot as the second witness. Lots of laughter. I bet that fun couple in the hot air balloon will last even if they go in for more extreme adventures later.

But today it's a wedding. Tomorrow is a funeral. Next week, a naming-day and commitment ceremony. Plus I've got a voice- over to record in the Melbourne studio for a new chocolate commercial. Billee, my agent rang me this morning. Hope they have a few samples for the actors.

'Wreath with lots of greenery ordered for tomorrow?' Violet from 'Infinity Blooms' checks. 'All prepared. I'll deliver in my trike bike basket. Makes it hard to fit in any cycling otherwise.'

'Yes. 2pm funeral in chapel. Mr Patrick Murphy,' I reply. 'Likely to attract a few extras.'

Generous Irish liquid hospitality at the wake always attracts more mourners.

The funeral arrangers have their preferred list of 'reliables', celebrants who won't embarrass them in public, and who can be diplomatic with upset families. But must be available at short notice. Relieved to be on their list.

'Are you available Quinn?'

'Of course.'

As the celebrant, best to stay a little removed professionally. Listen. Advise. Co-ordinate the ceremony. I make sure my client is looked after, even if other relatives have views on how things could be done differently. Smooth over any hitches. Fit around bossy wedding planners, a parasitic profession who rarely last long and the photographers who are just trying to shoot you.

But I'm daydreaming. Must concentrate on my current bride and groom.

'Quinn, you're needed for the photo with his parents!' the bride was insistent. 'With the F.O.G and the M.O.G. '

'Do you do stand-up comedy?' asks the father-of-the groom as the bride insists I join the group photo with the in-laws and all the vintage 60-ish bridesmaids in soft green, ankle length skirts and pretty bouquets of cottage garden flowers each with a single yellow chrysanthemum. My 'celebrant' reversible jackets are versatile with changeable cuffs and passable for funerals.

I stand at the back.

'No,' I reply.

'Pity. Have you ever considered it? Such a lovely ceremony you did. Entertaining too. Loved the garden theme.'

'Thank you. The bride and groom must take credit for that.'

'And our labels. I prefer D.O.G. (Dad of Groom) to F.O.G.'

I don't blame him.

And I'll have another word to Violet about the meanings of the flowers with difficult spelling. Luckily no-one else noticed. A yellow chrysanthemum signifies neglected love or sorrow.

Red would have been better.

The afternoon light falls through the window like a spotlight on the bride.

The yellow chrysanthemum flowers stand out. That's a worry.

'Do you have any gardeners or people knowledgeable about plants in your family?'

The F.O.B shakes his head.

That's a relief.

I nod and move to the side of the chapel once the group shot is done.

I'm not a stand- up comic, although one of my colleagues does Elvis and Star Trek themes. Not sure how he costs his 'celebs' events and decides how one 'personality' is more expensive as a celebrant. The number of words, price of the outfit or what the market will pay determined by the size of the family budget? I prefer to be moderate in my prices. He claims his 'shy' couples love having a flamboyant wedding performance organized by him in costume. Footy-fan themes are not my favourites although the club songs are often used as stirring exit music but brides or the deceased in footy scarves would not be my choice. My Dad's music was an exception, even if I used the wrong version. And definitely not the celebrant in a footy jumper. Nor a beloved club football in the coffin with the deceased but the client's wishes take priority. My approach is to smile for the camera, but let the client be centre stage.

Often the reception is hours after the ceremony.

Usually I leave just after the bride and groom head off to have their photos taken.

But recently I've become an inadvertent sleuth. Things went seriously wrong. I lost a client. Flora, the Tawny Femme Formidable.

Well, being a celebrant is a tight market and your reputation matters for future bookings and income, but it wasn't that kind of 'dissatisfied client' loss. Believe me, I've dealt with Bridezillas and prospective mothers-in-law from Hell. Not to mention feuding kidults with a hormonal imbalance of entitlement who want to be considered centre of attention as the favourite child even if they are middle – aged with a maturity by-pass.

But the case of Flora was challenging. Accident? Murder? I'm still unsure. Two serious suspects. Disinherited adult children who felt entitled to everything and a may-be scam lover both with the potential to be affected by her wedding and change of will. Timing was vital.

Flora and Her Much Younger Man

Flora had been a resident of Unit 1 since the 'Everest Residential Village' opened. But now she had a 'much younger' male companion. Some thought she'd been 'conned' and there was a dating scam involved.

I admired the way she didn't let her age and walking stick restrict her into the stereotypical 'doddery older woman'. Who else would have a champagne glass holder on a walking stick alongside her warning bell? Or walk her claimed 10,000 steps every day without cheating on her digital wristband counter?

'Do your 10,000 steps today Quinn?' Flora winks at me. 'Or did you adjust your wristband …like Art does?'

My long term partner Art and I had a short-lived fitness regime of walking and running daily. The problem was he announced it on his local radio program as 'sports news' fashion, hoping to attract some sports sponsorship for community programs. Didn't happen. So now the entire community monitors our lapses. Exercise is talked about more than done.

'A few more steps after dinner, to make up today's quota,' I say, unwilling to admit my low figures on today's tally.

Flora was so well organized, her entire wardrobe was tawny colour- coded in autumnal flowing jackets, lounging pants (her upmarket tracksuit equivalent) and her signature LONG scarves. Well- cut hair was streaked to match and her roots never showed. She used to be a tall woman but had shrunk a little with age. Privately I called her 'The Tawny Femme Formidable'. But her weakness was her family. Saying 'No' to them was hard because she'd come from a poverty-stricken refugee childhood herself, and wanted to give them all she had missed.

How did I know this about Flora? Art is a good interviewer and he often seduces his radio subjects into revealing more than they intended during his 'In Conversation' program. But he also pre-records for Channel Zero and offers the opportunity to delete and withdraw if interviewees have later qualms. Flora deleted, but I heard the original, unedited version in the studio during recording

'Tell the listeners about your reasons for choosing to live in this community?' is Art's standard opener.

After explaining about investing in 'The Village' partly because her family lived in the area, Flora had second thoughts. She was aware her children might hear the local program. And that gossip would exaggerate her property interests and disappointment in her children. And she hadn't even mentioned her 'younger male companion' whom we know about anyway. And which makes her of special interest.

'Delete it Art. Sorry you wasted your time.'

Momentarily, Art looks surprised but then covers his frustration at wasting his time. Only later he tells me he was a bit annoyed, but at work, he's always professionally polite.

'That's ok Flora. Your privilege. And I enjoyed hearing your story anyway.'

Art interviews on and off the record for Channel Zero the only community media outlet in town, plus freelances on webcam security because he's excellent at all kinds of recording.

My sister Bea caters for every function when more than one or two vegans, fructose intolerant or eating disorders are gathered together. So it's hard to keep a secret in this small town. A shared iced coffee or camomile tea at SAGE Café becomes a relationship or even a wedding by the time the eavesdroppers have relayed the rumour and got a few things wrong.

Or an ambulance parked outside any unit can be wrongly or correctly broadcast as another death. Indirectly Violet's 'Infinity Blooms' business does well out of the malicious gossipers who are occasionally forced to send flowers as a way of apologizing. Violet has pot plant 'Apology Specials' as she privately calls her sideline.

'My pot plants are doing better than my roses this month,' says Violet.

So there's lots of gossip mongering: innocent and occasionally destructive. And I think Flora was wise to pull that radio interview, because her new relationship with Dale became the subject of increasing gossip.

'Heard about Flora's new toy boy?'

Facts are hard to check. Especially about an attractive male nurse, who becomes a magnet for all the Village females, staff and residents. Including Flora, the octogenarian who still enjoys a sexual companion.

'My name is Dale.'

Dale is a well qualified male nurse, with the comforting reassurance of a caring manner, sympathetic eyes and the medical knowledge to deal with emergencies. Great insurance for anyone getting older. A professional carer. Or was he a con-artist? Lonely, wealthy women can be very vulnerable. Maybe I was overly- suspicious because I always watch the body language. Part of the on-going acting craft. Pretend care and genuine concern are difficult to distinguish in the short term. Dale was hard to read. His slight accent was intriguing. South African or Dutch?

And he was solicitous about his patients and the other residents.

'Would you like some extra help with that?'

Flora fell for romance. A last fling. With the blond male nurse, 30 years her junior with craggy, filmstar looks. And younger than all five of her adult children.

'Dale is wonderful.'

Falls are common in older age. That's why Everest has ramps not steps as part of their safety mission statement shown in their glossy brochure. Reassuring for 'Elders', the new, respectful word for old which has replaced 'vintage' in sales catalogues for aged care facilities.

'Take my arm,' offers Dale.

The elderly, which I've noticed means anyone older than the person speaking, are scared, not of falling, but of the subsequent inconvenience of plastered limbs, walking frames or moon -boots smelly from scruffy skin-flakes. Plus extra doctor and physio appointments.

But Flora 'fell' for nurse Dale.

'Like your 'Land of the Midnight Sun' tag on your walking stick, Flora.'

'Dale bought it on E-bay,' admits Flora with a grin. 'Haven't been there, yet.'

'E-bay?'

Flora smiles. She likes to pretend she's not familiar with some words and systems used by younger generations, but she is.

'Dale is keen on selling and buying artwork and limited editions on E-bay.'

I wonder how he affords those on a nurse's salary?

Sticks with symbolic tags for places visited have become the 'Elders' fashion accessory which Flora embraces too. Proud that Dale had bought her a gift of something symbolizing adventure.

Probably that's another reason why I liked her. Always been keen on Scandi Noir mysteries myself and love the bleak settings. The weather is almost a character. Often wear a fleecy vest while watching or reading the icy mysteries. Pretend I'm the sleuth and those plots are always tied up so cleverly at the end, unlike our messy village mysteries here which have 99 versions of the 'crime' depending upon who you are chatting with. Noir means crimes of moral ambiguity in dark surrounds and then things get worse. Bit like the Village really, except for the temperature. Village Noir could be a new genre. Fancy myself as observant, but got a few things wrong this time in Flora's case. Like motives and reasons.

I love complex role-play card games with twisted motivations. Our group meet once a month in SAGE Café and play 'Motives' all Saturday afternoon, unless I've got a wedding. My sister plays occasionally, especially as her husband Dan is away overseas with the military. We're both keen on games. Probably because our family played cards when we were kids, but 'Motives' is in another dimension. 'Aspies' love it but if you're not on the autism spectrum, like me, you need to be careful about using that word with the community. A bit like 'queer' and gender words if you're not part of the group. I love being no gender for an afternoon.

You become the super-hero, action character, in another time world, to which the opposing players keep dealing complications. Like no sight. Liabilities such a wearing restrictive clothing like armour or wings. Or losing your memory. Time limits. Or penalties for using your favourite word. Or bonuses like being able to fly. Or run in marathons without training. That really appeals to me. And then you have to play your hand to reach the goal you are dealt. Lots of different level packs. We're up to the abstraction goals in the spiritual pack like Nirvana or Enlightenment. Quite addictive. Sort of brain playing. Even if you're agnostic like me. They're even having a LONG PLAY Tournament soon, so we can play for several days. I think the challenge is remembering all the different parts allocated to the character you are playing. And having a laugh when you forget. Quite companionable.

Art says 'Motives' tends to attract obsessives. He's right, but it's a kind of parallel social life with like-minds. And I get to see my little sister.

'Quinn, I want to ask you something private. Could you drop by later this afternoon, about 5pm?' Flora requests.

So I did. Art and I live outside the Village, but just a few streets away in a rented place. Ours is the 'reno delight' which needs some work, especially on its street appeal. That's why the rent is low.

Walking distance away. I glance at my exercise wristband. Still a few thousand short of today's target. I won't share that with Art. If I were a super-hero playing 'Motives' I could achieve those steps in a single bound.

Unit 1 is bigger than the other residential flats with a slight incline for Flora's drive leading down to the basement double garage with the roller door which works on a remote. There's an internal door from her garage via stairs to her unit but mainly she enters by her own front door because of the easier ramp and she often parks on the driveway.

Unit 1 and 3 share a double garage.

Each unit has its own garage but Flora's neighbour Rocky doesn't use a car anymore. Lost his licence.

They've come to an arrangement, and Flora's visitors park in the second garage.

It is not quite 'living behind the shop' because most residents didn't know she was the owner of the entire estate. But if the Channel Zero interview had been broadcast, they might have been. This keeping quiet means Claud the manager has to deal with everyday complaints, not Flora. The delegation works, mostly.

Claud visited often but surprisingly no-one gossiped about that. They thought the manager's visits were related to constant complaints about theft from grumpy neighbour Rocky's rock garden. The Body Corporate likes uniformity with the residents' units but Rocky keeps adding his rocks and claiming it is 'street art'. After each major complaint, he removes a few. The fake-geologist has painted most of his gold nuggets and claims he has a fortune in the ground. Most of the theft was in his head. But the rocks were on the increase again with big engraved labels, often with the scientific names wrongly spelled. I notice spelling. That's why Violet always asks for my help with flower words at Infinity Blooms.

All communities have one really irritating neighbour, and Rocky at Unit 3 was it.

'Street art' was part of Rocky's ongoing Body Corporate battle which gave him an interest. Locals called it 'the graveyard' or Fool's Gold. Claud worried that he'd never be able to re-sell that unit because of the heavy lifting and cost involved in relocating the 'geological specimens' left by Rocky.

I looked at the awkwardly labelled mineral garden and

remembered overhearing Claud's wry suggestion after the last complaint.

'How about some rock music? Or a sound and light show with spotlights? Your electricity bill might go up a bit.' Claud suggested. 'Of course we'll watch it for you. Just getting new security web cams.'

Unit 3's got 'rocks in his head' was the local consensus.

But collectors' passions give meaning to empty lives, even if others consider them junk. And he liked being called Rocky as a nickname by other residents. As a kind of 'expert' acknowledgement, he thought.

We all have delusions. Mine are more modest, that I'll attempt a half -marathon and finish in under a week. Or win Celebrant of the Year (there isn't one yet).

Meanwhile residents sympathised with Flora's problem of living next door to Rocky AND with her demanding grandkids always asking to be bailed out of their traffic fines, accidents or other mistakes. Just as I arrive, grandkid Zac, the 18 year old storms out of Unit 1, slamming the front door, so hard, the windows rattle. He yells.

'It's NOT fair Gran. If you won't pay this fine, I might lose my licence and the car! It wasn't my fault that idiot crashed into me. And I've dropped out of the stupid course! The dog came out of no-where. I didn't meant to kill it and my car is uninsured. So I left. There's a lot of panel beating and spray painting needed.'

'No,' said Flora. 'Not this time. Go sort it yourself. Report it to the police station. Find out who owned the dog. Go and see them.'

'What? You won't pay for the damage to my car? Like… you bought the latest model for yourself last week and can't even use the remote. Unreal. Like. I won't have any wheels.

How will I get around? Girls won't go out with me. Can I borrow your wheels?'

'NO! Clean up your own mess. You go to the police station yourself.' Flora's voice was indistinct now behind the slammed door, but her message was clear. This cashed-up grandmother had said 'No' and meant it.

Best to stay out of family arguments. I'm not that involved with kids and don't really have any desire to have my own. I wait a minute, deciding whether to leave, but then knock. Flora opens the door.

'You heard? Sorry about that, Quinn. Family problems, again.'

Flora was not a victim of elder abuse. She was in charge and had choices. And I wasn't deliberately eavesdropping. Gangling, loud teenagers with aggression issues are hard to ignore. And they want to be noticed. But they cause emotional damage and drain energy.

'Decision time,' says Flora firmly. 'Come in.'

The clues existed (which may have contributed to her death) but I didn't put them together then. Talking about grandkids' achievements real and imaginary is the 'currency' of old age. Flora worried about the pattern of entitlement AND the lack of skills as her grandkids 'dropped out' of most courses in the syllabus. So she didn't mention them too much in conversation. Even Zac who was her favourite.

She'd given up on her own adult children. But others knew her offspring spent money they never earned; driving cars they'd never paid for. I suspected she'd propped them up financially so many times, thinking each crisis was 'this last time'. One daughter had already faced bankruptcy. Zac's latest hit-and-run episode was the decider for her. And there was no way she was loaning her new car to her grandson. He'd been caught 'joy-riding' before.

'Iced tea?'

Flora pours from a crystal jug with clinking ice. I prefer coffee in a mug, but as I sipped, I felt a bit embarrassed. She knew, I knew, too much about her family via Art's recorded interview, which as promised, he hadn't broadcast. Art does keep his promises and I rely on that too. But it was just one of those vulnerable moments, when a crucial decision was made, and Flora was talking to herself as much as to me.

'It's not a secret that my company owns Everest. The paperwork is public and my name is listed. But I don't talk about it, unless someone asks me directly. Not like that 'Undercover Boss' TV program. Everest is running well. I don't need to go undercover to be filmed as a pretend employee to find the faults. I have my own security systems in place. But family is another matter. And mine needs fixing with tough love.'

'In what way?' I ask.

'When you've made your own way out of poverty, there's a satisfaction in building a business which creates jobs and makes something that a community values. My kids have never felt that satisfaction. Or responsibility for their actions. And I want them to experience that. So I've had an appointment with my lawyer and there are a few papers I'd like you to witness.'

'Why me?'

'You're not family. Nor a beneficiary. And you've known me for a few years which is necessary for witnessing. And I went to that University of the Third Age class that Art ran about writing family history. Impressive.'

Flora likes the stimulation of younger, male company.

And Art can be charming. I know. In public, and even in private, when he's home. Sometimes I wonder what he sees in me because our relationship seems a bit unbalanced. I don't exactly fit the girlfriend role.

Apart from Channel Zero, Art is a 'geni' as genealogists like to call themselves. So he's popular with the residents of 'The Village'. What's now history was a current affair for them, to be recalled with nostalgia. All his research and popular 'freebies' talks are another reason we struggle to pay our rent. Art can't say 'no'.

'What interested you most?'

Flora replies, 'Art talked about economic patterns. Family dynasties with flaws. One generation builds up a business and the next lets it run down or destroys it. '

'Art dropped out of law school. And his family ice cream business. Dairy farmers originally. International iced sweets now.'

'Ah. Sounded like he'd had personal experience. Opting for community over corporate. A principled young man.'

Easy to say if you don't struggle to pay the rent. And his family not accepting Art's partner made it a gender issue. Maybe time to mention that.

'More to do with them not accepting me as Art's partner,' I suggest. 'His parents didn't want to know. We've only attempted once to explain about my being asexual. When they realized our relationship was long term, they didn't want us in the family business. Too embarrassed.

They preferred us to 'pass as a normal couple' is what his father said. 'Or it might be bad for business.'

'Oh.'

Flora is poised to ask another question, and then changes her mind, so I continue.

'I'm not a qualified lawyer either – Even though as a celebrant, I know about legislation like – the marriage act – adoption act – and privacy act. Art and I disagree about politics and lots of other subjects. And even disagree about beetroot in salad.'

The moment I said about the beetroot, I knew I sounded stupid and so trivial. But I was just trying to the change the mood. And Art hates beetroot but I like it. Fact.

Art also reads the financial reports for hours. His equivalent of my gaming analysis at 'Motives' card playing.

Flora looked at me as if she might have made a mistake in asking a favour of this idiotic beetroot-lover.

'Maybe I should have asked Art instead? '

'No problem, I'm happy to sign for you, Flora. And I've known you for at least three years. Is that long enough?'

Flora nods.

'All I need is a document witnessed and a little discretion about not mentioning this latest document to my children, yet.'

'Yes, of course Flora.' I slip back into formal celebrant role.

Sometimes you relax too much and assume you can be yourself, and then realize it's a mistake. Flora is a potential client, not a mate.

In 'The Village' most residents are experts on 'wills' because they change them so often. It is a kind of emotional blackmail to keep younger family visiting and staff attentive for favours. So we are used to witnessing the new versions, but witnessing only that the person was really them and knew what they were doing.

'Still got their marbles, 'is the colloquial term.

But most also know that a marriage invalidates any earlier wills unless there is a statement negating any future marriages.

Flora certainly did. A woman savvy enough to build up a property portfolio in the millions, knew a bit about contract law. So why hadn't she got her own highly paid lawyers to witness the documents? Was this a last minute change she wanted to put into place due to recent family reactions? Or something about which she was doubtful, wanted to keep in reserve, and could later deny?

'I want to control what might happen after my death,' Flora pulls out a fat, legal, cream envelope with a law firm inscribed on the outside. 'And how Everest will be run.'

Art and I were not in Flora's financial world. Even paying our rent was a challenge with my erratic work. Art's tendency to tell 'humorous personal news' on air, like our fitness failures wasn't enough to increase the limited audience of sponsors for his programs. Our income almost balanced our outgoings this month. Art was great on money theories, not practice. Luckily he was honest and Flora knew that.

'Art tells it the way it is.'

Meanwhile, ours was a country town doing it hard. A couple of factories had closed or re-located. Several families had left or the males had become FIFOs (fly in fly out) workers at interstate mines or offshore rigs.

'I don't want the major employer in a small country town going out of business. I know how many families depend upon 'Everest' employment. And my son Ed finds it impossible to get up before midday. How would he run the companies?' says Flora. 'And my daughters have no skills. Just short-lived ideas which never turn into businesses.'

'Why did Art's talk interest you so much?

'Someone asked about charitable trusts and matching interests. Reminded me that it might be possible to change my will in a way I hadn't considered before. Or at least force my family to consider changing the way they live.'

Big paintings covered the walls of Flora's unit. A few landscapes which looked old fashioned with gum trees and purple mountains. One wall looked like portraits of a younger Flora and I wondered if they had been commissioned. Or was she the recipient of artists' gifts? Could be embarrassing if you hated what the artists painted. One was a very abstract Flora with multiple faces, like a Picasso gone feral.

Flora noticed me looking at the feral painting. 'Do you recognize me? Painting was my previous hobby.'

I assume she means before Dale.

'Er. Your name is signed on the painting.'

'Self portrait.'

'Memorable.' This is my all -purpose comment when I haven't a clue what to say. Art classes in the Village and elsewhere produce some shockers of paintings, but keep tutors employed and students occupied. Fair enough. I change the subject.

'Notice you're a bit of a book collector?'

'I like first editions,' Flora admits. 'Like the smell of the paper.'

I always check bookshelves if older clients still have them after downsizing as they keep only the things significant to them. Often information is digital-only in the homes of younger families. But all offer clues to understanding family dynamics.

Not many family photos on Flora's shelves. Couldn't see any weddings photos of Flora's earlier partners. But sometimes females 'retire' those to inside drawers, if a new male is on the scene

Often photos clutter entire corridors in small flats, and

the re-arranged and often fictionalized past, takes over the present.

Others have 'forests' of feature photo walls of family trees in miscellaneous frames which have to be pruned or grafted as extra branches are chopped off or added.

My personal view is that it's the single 'oldies' who are keen on finding their ancestors and who take up the role of 'geni'. Those who still have real family living around them find that experience sufficiently draining not to want any more. Like Flora.

'I've got a pen for you.' Flora brings out some papers. 'Do you mind?'

'Marriage invalidates most earlier wills.' I say quickly. 'But a new baby may just put another beneficiary into the mix –.'

'At 80 plus, I'm not planning another pregnancy.' Flora's eyes crinkle into smiley wrinkles. 'No intention of being a medical marvel. I'm a little beyond IVF, although I still buy shares in medical research.'

We both laugh and the tension goes.

'Where do you want me to sign? In duplicate?'

I'm sure she knows what she's doing. And that it really is her, Flora. So I witness her signature on already drawn up documents and date them, with the same pen. Her fingers seem a little stiff as she writes. But I don't read the content. She relaxes a little and folds the documents into the envelopes.

'You wanted to ask me something else, Flora?'

'Quinn, would you act as celebrant at our wedding next month?' Flora requested in her tawny voice, rich with suggestion that any request she made would be agreed upon. And sounding relieved. It was as if she'd switched from family worries to negotiation mode at which she was always competent.

'Your wedding?'

'Yes, to Dale. You may have met him around the Village. He's the nurse who started here a few months ago. He's moved in with me. You might have seen his car in my driveway or in the street.'

Dale was respected by the other staff because he was a good worker. He was prepared to take extra and unpopular shifts. The older women liked his manners and his mellifluous voice. I still do occasional voice- over jobs as an actor. My voice is trained but Dale's was exceptional. Rich like thick honey. Recently he'd started Gentle Exercise classes for residents. 'Eye-candy' appeal as one resident described the booked out classes. Part of the reason for the escalating fashion in walking sticks with adventure place -tags is the exercise instructor, Dale.

'Yes, of course I'm willing to be your celebrant.'

The extra job was welcome. But anything to help Flora who'd been generous sponsoring Art's short-run programs.

A knock at the front door.

Flora smiles as she rises from her chair in a smooth, practiced movement, leaving her stick against the wall. 'Going to Gentle-Exercise class. Got to keep up with my young husband-to-be.'

Dale is at the door. I wonder how much he had heard. And if 'a few months' residency in Unit 1 qualified him for the six months needed for a de facto to inherit? And if he was living here now, why had he knocked?

'Forgot your key?' asked Flora. She was proud of Dale being part of her household and wanted me to know that. 'Spare is on the key hooks, just inside the door.'

'Thought you had visitors and I didn't want to interrupt,'

said Dale. 'Hi Quinn. Heard about the card games down at Bea's café. Need any more players?'

'Motives' gaming is a bit more complicated. Ever played it?'

'I used to fill in at bridge at my last job. If the residents were short of a player. We had a considerable turn-over there. Quite a churn rate. '

Not the most tactful thing to say in front of your elderly fiancée in the residential village she owned.

'What are the rules for Motives?' Dale asks. I'm suspicious of those who show instant, fake enthusiasm on the spot for the current subject, and have forgotten by the next time you meet. Could Dale be one of those?

'Drop in some time and watch, 'I invite, but I am just being polite. We don't really like observers. Prefer being a bunch of atypicals who like to get involved in other fictional action worlds without the criminal consequences of the real world. Tune-out time. Playing heroes with no specific gender who perform amazing acts. A change from living genderqueer in a society where you are considered different.

'Look out for that step Flora,' advises Dale as he winds her trailing scarf across her shoulder 'Might need your trainers for the exercise class. Would you like another iced coffee later?'

Dale looked genuinely fond of his older bride-to-be. Some relationships seem to be about energy rather than age. At first I thought this was one of those. Later I was unsure.

Runaway Ring Dog

'Benedict is part of our family. Would it be okay if he were the ring bearer?'

'Has he agreed?'

I always try to accommodate the clients' wishes.

'Benedict doesn't speak.'

'I can provide Auslan signing services.'

'Benedict is our fur baby. He's a dog.'

I look at this eco-friendly couple who are 'sort-of' organising their wedding rehearsal. Neither wear watches and they seem to live in a time vacuum of weather seasons, not digital minutes.

'Is it 10 o clock? Oh, sorry I forgot the time we arranged for the rehearsal,' says May the bride, a vague but friendly thirty-something with very straight, shiny hair, long enough to sit on.

They are 'dog' people. I am not. But I am the celebrant and it is their wedding.

'OK. We might need to rehearse the dog's role as part of the ceremony in your garden.'

This ceremony is to be in the bush garden of their eco-shack, beside a lake backing onto the national forest. In the past few years, they've extended the shack with their own mud- bricks, used solar panels, have rainwater tanks and grow their own organic food. So their seasonal timetable has been effective. SAGE café is catering for their alfresco wedding breakfast, using their home grown vegetables and eggs from their hens which all have names like Peace and Tranquillity. I was introduced to them too during the 'conducted tour'.

Chicken will not be on the menu.

'Which tree would you like to use for the ceremony?' I ask. 'We need room for the white foldable table holding the official papers and space for the bridal group. And having some kind of shade for your guests is helpful just in case the weather changes quickly. Best to be prepared for sun or rain.'

'It will be fine. I always get the weather right,' says the bride.

Her groom nods. 'She does.'

'Got the rings?'

'The best man has. He'll be here very soon. He's always on time.'

Using a pet as the ring- bearer and fastening the jewellery to his collar is a risky move. Then comes the challenge of getting the rings off at the right moment. Perhaps delegate?

'Maybe the best man can tie the rings on the dog?' I suggest. 'And get them off too?'

The bride nods. 'Tom is a policeman. He's very practical. Great choice for a best man.'

At least they didn't want the dog to be best man. That's harder to organise, especially as a witness signing the marriage certificate.

Witnesses are not required to be IN the bridal party – but if a dog is involved, …I need someone else, outside the bridal party who can sign. You can work out the maths % of canine and human.

Before the rehearsal, I look warily at the yard. It's one of those 'going-to-be-wonderful' eco-projects which is never quite finished. Using recycled material is excellent for the planet, but junk piles tend to accumulate.

'What will you use the iron bath with the claw foot for?' I ask.

'Outdoor chairs. Cut it in two. When I've got some spare time,' says the groom who has a very long name but is known as Theo.

Getting married and having a home-wedding is a higher priority than making outdoor furniture from old baths. Fair enough. The guests can stand for the short ceremony. Or sit on the logs Theo is positioning.

'We'll do a quick tidy up and make-over of the yard before the ceremony,' reassures the groom as I look at an old door leaning on the unpainted fence.

'Might be a good move Theo, so there's enough room for the guests and the catering tables.'

'It's taken us fifteen years to decide to get married,' confides the bride.

Looking around the yard, I get the feeling they are not fast decision-makers but at least they have dreams.

The chickens are housed in a palace of stained glass from a de-consecrated church.

'St Christopher, patron saint of travellers and even finding parking spots. Used to be up the road, but then it was sold. And so were the furnishings. We cherish that glass we bought.'

Rainbow light filters into the henhouse. The hens look content and not likely to travel.

'The coloured light calms them down. They produce so many eggs. And we play music to them too,' says May. Theo nods approvingly. 'Jazz on weekdays and classical on Sundays.'

Behind their shack is a track, rarely used because the mountain is so steep and overgrown. Only a few birdwatchers or serious hikers go there. It's a wall of rugged bush with bird noises.

'We bought the shack from a family with young children who were a bit concerned about the remoteness when one of their kids needed regular medical care,' explains May. 'And there was some kind of accident here.'

But the access road to their shack from the main road is reasonable with only a few potholes. My sister Bea the caterer is relieved about that, because she has to bring in all the food in her van on the day of the wedding.

Meanwhile, there's the issue of the dog and the rings.

'What kind of dog?'

'Ex-police. A gift from Tom. '

'How big is he? '

'The dog or the best man? '

We all laugh. The bride giggles. Sunlight filters through the trees and the scrubby tomato patch and broken wires don't seem to matter so much. It's their life and they seem content with each other.

'You need to fasten the rings securely to the dog collar,' I suggest.

An agile, big dog could shake a ring free and swallow it. Might take a few days to reappear and some brides are unwilling to wear it then. Even eco-friendly brides with composting toilets.

Or the dog may run off and swim away into the lake or bite the celebrant.

'This dog needs to be part of the rehearsal too,' I warn. 'Can you introduce us?'

Couples who have lived together for some time before the wedding, often have a pet who is a substitute child.

Benedict was a baby substitute.

An enormous baby.

One of his ancestors was a Great Dane.

Proudly the couple bring out Benedict, or more accurately Benedict pulls them behind him on a leash. Beautifully crafted leatherwork is one of the groom's saleable skills and he sells everything he makes at local markets. Theo made the very strong dog leash.

'Quinn, meet Benedict.'

I look at his teeth. Big teeth. Big dog. Big problem.

They are vegetarian but I suspect the dog is not.

'Will Benedict have a handler? Maybe your police friend? 'I ask. 'Just so he's ready when I need the rings during the ceremony?'

I carry insurance, but unsure if dog bites are covered. Might be in the small print I haven't read. I'm in the performance category of insurance which includes clairvoyants who should not need any insurance if their forecasting of the future is accurate. And there are the fire-eaters, stilt walkers and sword swallowers in my category. That is no comfort at this moment. I predict Benedict might disrupt the wedding and swallow something inappropriate.

I'm right to be wary. I'm no clairvoyant, just a celebrant who anticipates problems and tries to prevent them.

'He'll be perfectly behaved,' says the bride. 'Benedict must be part of our special day. I've got a white bow of ribbon for him. Look.'

'Let's see how he goes at the rehearsal,' says the groom, adjusting the dog's collar and clipping on a hand-made leather pouch. 'Shall I put the real rings in here? Or should we use a substitute ring just for the rehearsal, in case anything goes wrong?'

'Woof,' says Benedict.

I'm assuming that is a yes.

If the rehearsal goes badly, I always say,' The wedding

ceremony will be so much easier for you.' If it goes well, I say, 'There, that's what you can expect on the day.' Fascinating how it's the small things which worry them (and me) most. Like rings.

'Any kind of ring will do. It is not a legal requirement. Just a custom,' I reassure.

They settle on a couple of savoury biscuits as a ring substitute for the rehearsal. But the dog can smell the foody scent and eats them. By this stage the best man Tom has arrived.

So then they use the real rings in the beautifully crafted leather pouch

'There.'

'You could just tie them on with string to the dog collar,' Tom suggests, but the groom is sentimental about his leatherwork. Plus the entwined T and M, I just noticed on the ring bag.

Lost rings are the most common problem at weddings. Another celebrant told me she carries a spare pair to every rehearsal and wedding. And she has used them 4 times over twenty years. Maybe I should start doing that?

Best men get nervous, and forget where they put the rings. Often the rings are SO safe, they can't find them. Or the ring-bearer is a small boy who drops the ring at the crucial moment, and it rolls under the biggest piece of heavy furniture which has to be moved by three well muscled guests. That happened to me last year.

'Ready?'

Apparently Tom, the best man had worked with crime scene dogs that included Golden retrievers, Labradors, German shepherds, and Border collies commonly used as 'cadaver dogs.' But this failed, crime-scene dog Benedict was being recycled as a ring dog, for this wedding ceremony. A 'gift' which couldn't be refused, from the best man. Even a canine gift with Great Dane ancestry or at least one dog relative who was a Great Dane, judging by his size.

'Sit, Benedict!'

It took a few minutes.

'Benedict wasn't fast enough at responding to commands,' Tom explained. 'Not for police work.'

Luckily we had time to practise for the wedding.

Unluckily, he reverted to skills learnt at his previous training course and sniffed out bones of a body in the bush track behind where the wedding was to be held.

Bush settings are popular with bridal couples. A rural backdrop for the photos is appreciated, especially if the parents are from overseas or can't get to the wedding.

And this eco-couple wants to celebrate the natural setting of their home.

But the reality can be flies, heat and in this case, the finding of a dead body.

The 'make-over' of the yard had been a speedy transformation into a wedding setting. All their friends had helped. Recycled junk piles were covered with fairy lights. Lanterns hung from the branches. White bows marked the track into the yard. Animal poo had been recycled in the veggie garden. A mate had painted the fence so recently that the WET PAINT sign was still on.

'Don't lean against that yet. It'll be dry in time for the meal when we all sit down.'

Bea had done a brilliant job of catering for the wedding breakfast. Turned the discarded bath with the claw feet into an ice-filled bar of drinks including an exotic fruit punch from local fruit trees. Upturned the door into another table and covered with a bright yellow cloth.

Smells of cooking wafted. Finger food. Vegie sausages. Savoury mini pies using lots of eggs. Fruit platters with the bride and groom's intertwined initials written in strawberries.

'Our initials! And we can eat them!'

A wedding cake iced with the colours of the stained glass windows.

'Thank you so much Bea. I didn't know whether you'd be able to get the colours,' said the bride. 'I'll go and get dressed now. Theo has changed already.'

The veggie and fruit mocktails in red, orange, yellow, green, blue, indigo and violet look colourful as guests sip, waiting for the ceremony to begin. Bea has used rainbow-themed drinks once before in catering for a commitment ceremony. So successful, she's recycling the idea.

But Benedict the ring-dog is still the problem.

'Stay Benedict.'

He didn't.

Flustered by the noise and fairy lights, when Tom lets him off the leash, Benedict takes off. The rings are still in the leather pouch, even if bouncing around against the heavy neck of the dog.

He races up the track into the bush. He bounds out of sight, with the rings.

'Hey Benedict. Stop. Wait. Stay!'

Theo and Tom take after him. I follow but not quite at their speed.

It's an uphill sprint over branches and through gullies. I can't imagine we'll ever catch him. He's got four long legs, to start with. And the bush is dense, with occasional tracks.

I pant behind Theo. Tom is out in front, but the dog is out of sight.

We climb to the top of the ridge, and just below in the gully is Benedict. Scrubby bush. Patchy soil. Dense trees.

'Look.'

The three of us look down, panting.

Benedict is about ten metres below us. And there's another track behind him. He's sitting beside a mound of earth. I can't see if the leather pouch is still around his neck.

'Benedict. Stay!'

Theo shakes his head, 'Useless command. That dog has a mind of his own.'

We clamber down the slope and into the gully. Fallen trees litter the path. We climb over branches and get snagged on them. My arm is bleeding.

Benedict is sitting in scrub just off the track. Some of his earlier police training must have stayed with him.

He has been snuffling in the undergrowth, but the leather pouch is still attached to his collar.

'Got you.' Theo grabs the dog. 'And you've still got the rings.'

'No he hasn't! They've fallen out.' I check. 'Gone.'

'Benedict only waited because he's found something. Some bones.'

'What!'

'He's found some bones!'

'What sort of bones?'

Tom points at the mound beside the fallen tree trunk

'Looks as if something was buried here.'

Benedict is already pulling out one bone with his teeth.

'Drop it!' says Tom and the dog does.

'Maybe it's a body.'

Tom takes charge. 'Don't disturb anything. This could be a crime scene.'

ॐ

Although the signal doesn't work well on the mountain, Tom calls his police colleagues about the bones.

He takes some photos at the site and sends them through with the map co-ordinates.

The police respond immediately.

'They want us to wait while they check the visuals.'

'How long?' I ask, thinking of the wedding guests.

'If the celebrant and groom are missing, the wedding will have to start late.'

'I'm no expert, but those bones didn't look human,' says Theo. 'Not big or long enough.'

'I agree, 'says Tom. 'More like a big cat. Maybe a feral? Certainly not a kitten. Maybe a kangaroo?'

'I think it might have been a pet.' Theo says.' Probably the family that lived here before. With a sick kid, they didn't want the other children upset further. And a family buried it, so the children wouldn't be so upset. Heard there had been some kind of accident.'

'Why bury out here?'

'There's easier access from the other track over there,' Tom pointed.

'Yes, the father did tell me about their car reversing over the pet. I think the mother was driving. '

The mobile went.

Tom answers. 'It's ok for us to go then? Yes. I'll leave a marker. Thanks.'

Tom looks at Theo. 'Back to the wedding. We might need a change of clothes, mate. I'll hang onto Benedict this time.

❧

The leather punch is empty. Both rings have dropped out in the scrubby bush. But where? No more time left.

'Any spare leather in your workshop that could be used as a temporary ring?' I ask Theo.

'Of course. Come and choose what you want.'

I follow Theo inside the shack and notice a metal detector hanging with his tools. Tom notices too.

'Theo, is that the one you were going to use to find your fortune in gold nuggets?' asks Tom.

'No luck.' The bridegroom nods. 'But I've got a leather ring we can use.'

Guests are arriving. And even the fence paint is dry.

'Stay. Benedict. Drop.'

Benedict opens his huge mouth, but the Best Man holds him firmly.

The bride looks beautiful. The groom is now wearing his second best suit and the best man has tidied himself up. I have a Bandaid on my arm.

I cover all the formal words, get them to sign on the small table and pronounce them officially married.

Theo kisses the bride.

May looks down at her new, leather ring. 'Perfect' she says and looks so happy.

'Darling, if we ever find the other ring, you can wear them both,' says Theo.

❧

I had the idea about the substitute leather ring, but Tom had an even better idea about the metal detector.

The honeymooners had a plane to catch that night.

Tom and I went metal- detecting up the bush track after they left.

Took us five hours.

But we found one wedding ring PLUS some amazing metallic objects, including the spade used to bury the bones.

I was worried that spade might have been part of a crime.

But then the police confirmed that the bones were that of a huge kangaroo.

'Apparently the pet of the family with the sick child who used to live here. The father buried the animal away from the shack because the kids would have been upset to learn the mother had reversed the trailer over it. So the parents said the 'roo had run away.'

'This was before counselling customs that children be involved in grief ceremonies,' I suggest. 'Or rules against keeping pets of native species.'

'Maybe,' Tom agrees.' Probably an on- the -spot decision by an upset father.'

We didn't find the second wedding ring.

Currently I'm working on recycling my Quinn's 'Theory of Attraction 'for future weddings. 'Two people exert a force of attraction on one another known as ...' Substitute marriage or commitment for 'gravity'. Haven't quite sorted it yet. Not keen on the over-used 'soul mate'. Soul- mateship doesn't sound right. More fitting for drinks on a pub-crawl.

And I'd like to get the metallic attraction in there, somehow. Sort of a romance detector.

The Best Man is dog-sitting while the bridal couple is away.

I'm glad they didn't ask me to perform that ceremony for them.

Quinn's Theory of Attraction

A Romance Detector finds romance rather like a metal detector seeks gold- and can be observed in action when two people exert a force of attraction on one another and they are drawn to Romance.

A Driving Force

'Healthy active ageing' is the branding of 'Everest'.

Affairs are not advertised but many have 'companions', where the relationship started in the village. An 80 year old 'girlfriend' or a 77 year old 'boyfriend.' is not unusual. What is limited is the supply of older males. So staff and visitors are also eligible targets. Especially younger males.

'Why bother with marriage at 80 plus? Why not just move in together?'

'Why not live next door? You don't have to sleep together.'

'They want to.'

'A wedding is a social event,' says Claud. 'A chance to dress up. Good for local business. Flowers. Catering. Lawyers. Accommodation changes. Two singles who have been widowed moving in together or marrying is preferable to going alone into the hostel or units. Cheaper for them in terms of accommodation.'

'But not in other ways. Whose family gets what? Exit fees. Wills have to be changed. Witnessed.' I suggest. 'More complications. You know I'm not allowed to give legal advice as a celebrant, but clients ask.'

Claud and I chat often. We're both fixers. Enjoy problem-solving. I get his advice on 'renos' for our house. Not that Art and I have done much yet about our falling down fence or the bathroom plumbing. His parents are threatening to visit, so we'll have to tackle the 'renos' soon. I don't want another reason for them to criticise me as Art's partner.

Much easier to be compassionate about elders who are

not relatives. Can't do much about my gender preference but I can fix the fence. Well, sort of.

'If you don't know how much longer you have to live, and funerals have become your afternoon tea entertainment, why not have a few months or years of 'romance' and sharing companionship?' says Claud. 'It's a reason to get up in the morning.'

'Some 'funeral crashers' drop into funeral wakes knowing there will be a good feed – – they are easy to identify. 'funeral trolls' I call them. A few can be charmers as well as professional afternoon-tea eaters,' I say. 'Swell the numbers.'

'True.' Claud nods. 'How's Art's fence coming on?'

'Slowly.'

Quinn's Theory of 'Stuff Ups'.

'The most incomprehensible thing about the world is that it is comprehensible.'– is my all purpose Albert Einstein quote to explain any 'stuff-up'.

Apart from making sure elderly drivers are re-tested, and giving us free fence advice, Claud manages Everest which includes the retirement units and also the nursing home. Their versatile chapel is becoming familiar because I've performed a few funerals and the occasional wedding there. It's been designed for instant religion change of symbols from Catholic crosses to Buddhist with neutral drapes for Agnostic funerals.

Everest runs a tight business, under the Body Corporate with re-furbishing and resale and instant turnover once a resident dies. There's an administrative fee per year of occupancy, but the families do get some of the original money back. It's in their interests to have a high and quick return with a new tenant once their parent has passed away. I'm sure Flora's family is aware of that.

'Too many vacant units affects the re-sale price,' explains Claud. 'They all drop if there's too much choice. So we need new residents quickly. Churning it's called. '

Sounds a bit mercenary as a policy. But at the personal level, Claud is practical.

As manager, Claud is vigilant about money and reputation, his and that of the nursing home. Keeps a close eye on staff so there's no thieving from forgetful residents which does happen in other places. Residents of the high care area don't remember who borrowed from them and often blame others who haven't.

'Money is missing from my wallet!'

'No, your wallet is in the manager's safe. You don't need money here.'

There's a safety code on the locked door to keep 'wanderers' in the secure area of the nursing home. Family visitors forget and key it in front of patients, who wander out if their short term memory enables them to remember that day's code.

Sad aspect for a manager to deal with, but Claud is matter-of-fact. An ex-tradie, he can fix things in an emergency and supervised the recent security cameras.

Claud takes pride in doing a good job. Even if he cost-cuts at times.

Youth assume that the elderly are beyond passion. And that sex stops at your parents' age. Wrong. Energy and flexibility, not chronological age matters. Whether you can still drive or walk matters. How many topics other than how many pills you are taking that you can talk about. Octogenarian Flora was more active than most decades younger. And when living in a confined area, relationships matter. Ice cream social–dates at SAGE café. Barefoot Bowls. Bridge. Tai chi in the meditation park, near the Ever-Resting

Memorial garden where ashes were often scattered amidst the roses. All diplomatically included in the brochures.

Most of my wedding work comes by word of mouth. I average three ceremonies a week, mainly at weekends, 3pm Saturday is the prime time and the most expensive for the function rooms, but funerals have little warning, so I have to be flexible.

'Are you cancelling Motives again!' complains one of the players. This is our super-heroes, addictive card game which is increasing rapidly in popularity.

'Sorry. Unexpected ceremony. But you can play without me. Bea can play instead.'

'Says she's too busy with a vegan catering job.'

Weddings are planned at least a month ahead for the legal requirements. It's not just the 30 minutes of the ceremony; it's preparing the paperwork, attending the meetings before, the rehearsal and the 'being available to answer questions'.

My website videography has to be updated constantly. A new version of an acting portfolio is the way I regard that. In between I race off to Melbourne to do the odd acting role when my agent Billee gets me any. Been quiet lately, so I'm glad to have celebrant work. So my website is necessary. I get permission to use photos from wedding clients looking happy in various locations, but advertising funerals is a bit more of a challenge. Try to use flowers or symbols, but nothing likely to offend. That's why I was checking flower colours with Violet and what they mean in some cultures.

'Change the colour of your jacket for variety in the film clips,' suggests Art who helps me with the techie stuff. He films me speaking in 'The Village' against the rose garden in different coloured tops. That's how we recorded an inadvertent clue of Flora's new car being driven past. More about that later.

Weddings have their own language. Before I started working as a celebrant, I thought a D.O.G. was a 4-legged canine. Now it's an abbreviation in my running sheet for the wedding. It can mean Dad of the Groom, if your relative doesn't want to be called a F.O.G. Father of the Groom. But there's also S.O.B. which means Son of Bride in Flora's case.

Her workshy son Ed who never got up in time.

Art smiles. 'I thought S.O.B. that meant something else in Ed's case. Is he going to walk his mother down the aisle? Any competition for flower ladies amongst the Village residents?'

Art and I have another life that is nothing to do with the Village, even though we only live a few streets away, but sometimes we overlap. Art is always seeking interviewees for his community programs but he's avoided the 'rock man' neighbour of Flora. 'Nutter' is Art's opinion. A bit harsh when Art likes eccentrics, even 'wordy' ones like me.

The new term is 'flower ladies' for older friends supporting the bride. The flower ladies are not the ones putting blooms into the venue, as in the olden days when they 'did the flowers' for the church wedding. They are the 'vintage' bridesmaids, and in a retirement village, there's competition for that status. All like to be invited even if they reject the offer.

'Will you have any attendants Flora?' I was sorting the logistics for the chapel. 'Flower ladies? '

Many couples choose to go against tradition now – and have males on the bride's side – and girls on the groom's side – which can make it quite complicating for celebrants but I approve of the changes.

'Considering. Dale made a few suggestions.'

For himself or for Flora? He seems to have a number of lady friends.

Then we got to the paper work for the marriage.

'Your patients become your friends?'

'Yes.'

'And mention you in their wills.'

'I've been blessed in that way, several times.'

'You're good at remembering passwords.'

'Often my clients like me to do their withdrawals at the ATM, especially now there's no bank in the Village and they'd have to go into town.'

'Lots of unexpected deaths?'

'Statistically likely in the age group.'

'Have you been married before?'

'Yes.'

'We need to list the details.'

'There isn't enough space.'

Dale doesn't need to be an Australian citizen to get married, and I don't care what visa he's on – or if his visa has expired. Border protection would be interested but not me – and it doesn't prevent them from getting married. I've had a groom deported one week after getting married after I had submitted the legal paperwork to the registering authority, because he was an illegal immigrant.

Dale claimed he was born in South Africa and the paperwork was on its way.

My 'scam' alarm bell is ringing. Couples who meet via online dating agencies often have problems with missing work or residency visas and the wedding has to be postponed. I've had a few of those delays.

But Flora didn't seem worried. AND they hadn't met

online. Theirs was a vintage reversal of the 'office romance' between the Boss and a worker.

Marrying Flora would not enable permanent Australian residency for Dale. Marriage does not give permanent residency anymore.

Perhaps his earlier brides had other assets? Maybe he needed this wedding for reasons other than Flora's money? Acquiring a ready-made family didn't seem a likely motive. Perhaps it was love?

Dale had not yet suggested a best-man. With older marriages, often family were chosen but Flora's son didn't seem a likely best man. And gangling Zac was out of favour with his grandmother, since he continued joy-riding. It is possible to have a wedding without attendants, but there's sure to be competition for those roles once the news gets out. The ladies like to re-use their floral dresses. All like to talk about the weddings, before and after. A bit like young schoolkids and the status of who gets invited to which birthday party. What are you wearing?

Most use Skype to keep in touch with interstate or overseas family but also for romance locally. 'Can see her face and chat without having to walk too far.'

The male/ female ratio means any older man can choose his 'lady friend' from an array of residents.

'And what if two females want to move in together. Or two males? Does the Village have policy about same sex relationships?' Claud avoids that question on Art's 'In Conversation' program.

Occasionally Art tries to cover LGBTIQ subjects. Reactions in 'The Village' and in the wider country town are mixed. Quite a lot of talkback on same sex marriage or how forms could be filled in with an extra square if you don't wish to tick only the male or female option. A few critics with strong views against employment of trans or gay people but that's more a local issue of declining jobs anyway. 'Art, why are you wasting time on radio talking about people like them!'

Ironic.

Art and I must be 'passing' well even though his parents disagree.

Art and I are not highly visible as a diverse gender couple, and as we live in the mainstream community, most think we're a hetero couple if they think about it at all.

Existing 'Village' residents lift their charm game when a newcomer arrives. But ironically this time the problem was not a new female but rather the male nurse-carer Dale. All the women wanted him to look after them. And the men too.

'Dale, do you have a moment?'

And he appeared to be keen to help, especially if they had financial assets.

Meanwhile, I had a different kind of con-artist challenge.

This Friday 13th ceremony, my recently deceased client had an Irish name. MURPHY is a give away. Irish music. And Violet's tastefully arranged greenery looked superb. Multiple shades and textures of green fronds. Infinity Blooms again.

Then the funeral trolls turn up.

'Were you a friend of Patrick?'

'Of course. But I haven't seen him for a few years.'

Seventy-ish with a drinker nose and wrinkled drip- dry shirt with a well used black tie.

I look around the foyer. They usually travel in threes. There were two more in their 'just respectable' funeral gear at the temporary bar. They check the funeral notices for ethnic names, because catering at those wakes is more generous.

The Irish have the most booze. And this widow was known to have agreed to an open bar.

'He was such a good bloke. Always willing to help anyone. Paddy was a good mate.'

'Patrick. My step-father's name was Patrick,' corrects the widow's daughter.

'Er, we knew him as Paddy.'

'Or Patsy…'adds the second Irishman, raising his glass.

'Patrick,' nods Irishman No 3 refilling his glass while dusting pastry flakes from his dark suit with the frequently recycled black tie.

Cheerful con men prepared to talk worlds of fiction to the widow about what a wonderful bloke her husband had been. And then they drink to his memory for the rest of the afternoon and the evening until the caterer packs up.

Quinn's Law of Hijacking Grief

When a neighbour or distant relative feels entitled to claim greater loss and more sympathy than the bereaved partner who is too polite to contradict. Also known as Enjoying Funerals at Others' Cost.

The cheerful Irish conmen are harmless but expensive. Some of the Everest ladies turn up regularly for all ceremonies run by a particular funeral parlour because, 'They have the best afternoon tea with scones, real raspberry jam and cream.'

A little different from the attitude of Flora's ungrateful offspring.

Flora's eldest son Ed corners me as I leave the chapel.

'Has my mother asked you to witness a new will?'

'New will?' I knew Flora was planning something, but I was not sharing information with the S.O.B., if his mother wanted to keep things quiet.

'Remember me. I'm Ed Nat, Flora's eldest son.' He puts

out his hand but I don't shake as I remember an earlier, abusive meeting. How could I forget him? Rude and totally self-obsessed.

'Now let's talk about you. What do you think of me?' is Ed's typical level of conversation.

I couldn't believe my ears the first time. Especially as he wasn't joking.

Months ago, I met Ed who qualified in 'hanging around,' and not much else. Until his mother announced the wedding, he had been waiting decades to 'inherit' and filled in time having holidays. Plus vacations and weekends away for a 'well deserved' break.

All Flora's ageing offspring fitted the maturity-bypass category. Five of them. AND their hangers-on and growing brood of children living rent-free in town in Flora's earlier mansion.

'Ed, are you going to give Flora away at the wedding ceremony?'

'No way. My mother has been my meal ticket for years. Now she wants to marry this male nurse who is 30 years younger. He's younger than ME! It's obscene to consider them together in the same bedroom.'

According to Violet, Flora's daughters had failed in all the ventures Flora had staked for them.

Daughter No 1 was the most disliked locally. Zac was her son. She always assumed she could charge up everything to her mother's account and local traders were fed up with chasing their money. Daughter No 2 was overheard to say. 'I wish she'd hurry up and die, then I'll go first class to Europe again.'

Ed asked, 'How long do you think she'll last? What was in the will you witnessed? Did I get it all?'

'Sorry, I have an appointment.' I leave, feeling annoyed with myself for apologizing even with this fake excuse. My only appointment was with the weeds in our front non-existent garden and I keep postponing that. Both Art and I dislike weeding so we rotate the unpopular jobs. He got the fence fixing (still waiting). Even pulling weeds was preferable to listening to Ed complain.

I've met a few toxic 'seenagers'; my term for rude seniors who act like teenagers, but this family was a 'ten out of ten' soap opera.

'God's Waiting Room for Oldies. Ever-Rest. 'Visitors always joked to residents about the choice of name of where they were living. But it had been inherited from a New Zealander keen on Sir Edmund Hillary's conquest of Mt. Everest.

Since an 'artist ', who will remain nameless, added a hyphen and a capital letter R to the official sign to read Ever-Rest instead of Everest at the front entrance, I've heard that 'God's Waiting Room' phrase a few times.

Agnostic, 83 year old Flora was NOT waiting for God. Especially when she could choose how she spends her time and with whom. But she'd decided to marry, which has legal implications.

And it wasn't her first marriage. She built up her own business after she was first widowed. Used to making decisions. But was this marriage decision strategic? Or a lapse of judgment by a normally shrewd business woman? Was it the first sign of failing mental abilities? Or was that an argument a disgruntled adult child like Daughter No 1 might wish to use to challenge any will in which she and her son Zac didn't feature?

'Why marry when you can just move in together? And have already.' I ask.

'Need to sort out the legal stuff. Not all my children were born within legal marriages.'

'You didn't marry their fathers?'

'Only the first two.'

'Will a family member walk you down the aisle, Flora?'

Best to be diplomatic. Unlikely for any of them to give away their source of unlimited credit. But I invited them.

'Do you all want to share in your mother's…big day?'

It was a tiny chapel. Even repositioning the pews, wouldn't enable six abreast on the aisle not with Flora's walking stick too.

I suggest a compromise.

'How about a relay? ALL walk Flora down the aisle to give her away to Dale, a few steps each?'

'Like a baton change, with me as the baton?' Flora joked. She really wanted this wedding and for her family to be involved without unpleasantness. But it wasn't going to happen.

'Not sure if I'll even be there,' says Daughter No 3.

'You're not expecting us to buy you and Dale a wedding gift, are you?' says Daughter No 4.'

Her offspring were ungracious about everything while Flora was trying so hard to have a family occasion.

I suggest, 'Why don't you agree amongst yourselves on the best solution. If you can't decide, I'll organize it. Draw lots.'

Since they found it impossible to agree on anything, I pull a name out of the hat.

'Daughter No 4' got the giving-away job. That was an unfortunately short-lived audition role.

ॐ

Meanwhile, Flora summoned all her family to Unit 1 on the night before the wedding rehearsal, to explain her changed inheritance plan.

I knew because she asked Art to discreetly record it for her and make some duplicates.

'A record for them to think about later, if they find it difficult to take in the details. Evidence even if not admissible in court because of possible electronic tampering…but they may not know that.'

'Don't you want your lawyer present, Flora?' Art suggests.

'No. I like to do things my own way. Let's see how things play out. Maybe they'll have a sufficient shock and I won't need the lawyers.'

Flora's extended family crowded into her lounge room. Even Zac walked there: a new experience for him. I heard about this later, from Art who was secretly recording, at Flora's request.

After serving her usual iced tea and savoury nibbles (today's SAGE café special), Flora sat enthroned with her 'Land of the Midnight Sun' stick hung on the back of her arm chair. She spoke clearly, with a sense of occasion, and the hidden camera in the pot plant recorded it all.

'At 83, I'm aware I won't live forever. I want to leave each of you a legacy. '

'That's a relief,' sighed Ed. 'Thought you were going to leave everything to Nursie-boy.'

Flora ignores him. 'Dale and I are getting married within the month. Marriages revoke all earlier wills. Just because you marry does not give rights to half – that is something the magistrate would work out pro rata – depending on the number of other beneficiaries and the time we've been together. So as my husband he would be entitled to a percentage. Dale has rejected this.'

'I bet he has. Probably wants the lot,' mutters Daughter No1.

'The legacy I want to leave each of YOU is involvement with a charity of your own choice. However I have a few conditions.'

There was a collective gasp and then an outburst.

'You're cutting us out of your will!'

'What do you mean an involvement? Do we control the money?'

'No. You contribute time,' says Flora.

'But what about our right to inherit?' asks Ed. 'As your dependent children?'

'Dependency usually cuts out at 18 years. No longer a minor then.' Flora looks across at Zac who shrugs.

'You'll be inheriting the opportunity to work. You'll still have somewhere to live. The mansion in town where you are currently living is to continue to be shared by all of you. Seven bedrooms, four bathrooms and two kitchens is enough for most families. Rates and utilities are paid. And outside the Village, there are a few shop leases also. Income from those will go to you.'

'What happens to the rest of your money?' asks Daughter No.1.

'I'll spend it on Dale and myself. We intend cruising indefinitely. All around the world, with meals, entertainment and laundry provided. Plus frequent changes of scenery. Scandinavia first for our honeymoon, then Alaska and the Arctic. '

There was silence.

'Cool,' says Zac. 'You won't need your new car then.'

'Are you joking?' asks Daughter No.2.

'No. Each of you is to nominate a charity NOW that you favour. The money that you had thought was coming to each of you will go into a charitable foundation to support that project. You have naming rights on the project if you wish.'

'Don't know much about charities,' mutters Ed.

'That's partly why I'm doing this. Will give you a lifetime interest.'

'You mean like a hobby?'

'No! An occupation.'

Flora turns to her grandson. 'Since you are overly keen on fast driving and cause frequent accidents. I've put down the Para Olympic Games as your nominated charity. Enable you to appreciate how others overcome limitations.'

Zac gasps, 'Unreal.'

'The Smith Family helps families down on their luck. Might give you an insight into budget reality, 'Flora nods to Daughter No. 1. who shrugs. Then Flora turns to her second daughter. 'You are so good at losing money in small businesses that a mentoring scheme for young authorpreneurs may be an appropriate charity.'

'Not interested,' says Daughter No. 2. 'Why help them?

ॐ

Art turns down the live-feed audio. 'She intended Claud to do the day- to- day administration of the charities. Dale was to sponsor a charity too, if he wished.'

'Does Dale know that?'

'He wasn't at the family meeting. '

'Was that because he isn't family yet? Until after the wedding?'

'I think Flora just wanted to get the business over. And without quarrelsome adults insulting him, and her.'

'Adults? They act like toddlers. They won't turn up. Unfair to inflict them on the people needing help anyway! What if they refuse to get involved?' I ask.

'Flora covered that. Bribery. She's offering a lump sum each on retirement, linked to how many years they've been actively involved in their charity.'

'Don't think much of her chances.'

'And she put in a clause, that if any child of hers challenged the will after her death, they got nothing at all."

'Savvy lady. Even if that rarely stands up in court."

'No,' says Art. 'I don't think it will work. But the unlimited supply of money has been cut off. They get THAT message.'

'Why didn't she do it earlier?'

'We all put off difficult decisions.' Art fast -forwards to the end.

Ed turns and shakes his fist in naked rage, not realising he is recorded on camera. 'I'm your eldest son. I'm entitled to inherit and I'll challenge your will through every court, no matter what it costs in legal fees.'

'And what if you lose Ed? Who will pay your costs then? 'asks Daughter No 2.

Daughter No. 3 says, 'I'm not even going to use the name 'Mum' for her anymore. Mum has stitched us all up.'

Ed laughs bitterly, 'That didn't last long. You just used her name.'

Vintage Drivers and Infinity Blooms

Pension day, there was a bit of a traffic jam in the car park. The disabled parking bays were full, so drivers were wedging awkwardly at odd angles.

Being still able to drive was a status marker for residents. Failing eyesight or problems with headlights from oncoming traffic, meant night driving was the first to go. But now it was daylight and a beautiful sunny day. So those who were licensed to drive or even use the popular motorised scooters, were out and about.

Fred looks a bit awkward getting into the driver's seat of his vehicle parked outside the pharmacy shop window. Stiff and arthritic. A bit unsteady and slow getting his knees into the car.

Another car with indicators flashing is waiting to go into his space but Fred takes a while to get his seatbelt on and the key in the ignition. He turns and sees the other car waiting for his parking space.

He needs to reverse out, quickly.

Flustered, he puts his foot down.

The car jerks. But it goes in the wrong direction.

'Look out!' yell the bystanders.

The car careers forward across the pavement, hits the rubbish bin and stops centimetres from the pharmacy, alongside 'Infinity Blooms'. Another few centimetres and both plate glass shop windows would have been smashed.

Dr G2, the pharmacist rushes out to help in her white lab jacket and thick, black rimmed glasses. Fred is more embarrassed than hurt. Just a trickle of blood on his face from hitting the steering wheel. His eyes are dazed.

'So sorry,' he mutters. 'Just a mistake.'

'Must have thought your foot was on the brake Fred, and it was on the accelerator,' says the pharmacist who helps him out of his seat and they inspect the front of the car.

'No damage.'

She picks up the rubbish bin.

Kindly Dr G2, as locals called the pharmacist, looks after Fred. She knew him from his regular prescriptions. Her husband Dr G was the local doctor, but most patients couldn't cope with their long Indian surname, Gangopadhyaya, so they were known as Dr G and Dr G2.

If you're going to have an accident, best to crash into the chemist shop where the pharmacist is on duty. 'Especially the lovely Dr G2.'

Or that's what Fred told everybody for the rest of the week until Claud the manager organised that Fred be re-tested for his licence which he fails.

'Half-price concession taxi vouchers are possible,' Claud reassures. 'And a motorized scooter with a FRED number plate might be a safer option.'

The strip shopping street including the chemist, Bea's café and Violet's 'Infinity Blooms' and a few vacant shops is alongside the Village entrance and most residents use it as an extension of 'The Village'.

Claud arranges bollards to be erected along the pavement

to protect the shop fronts from erratic drivers. And paints the rubbish bins in bright safety yellow.

'Used to work in a seaside town. Bikie gangs rammed their vehicle across the pavement and smashed the wine shop plate glass window and took the booze. Bollards help protect the shopkeepers' businesses. We put some up there too.' explains Claud. 'But only after they'd taken all the beer.'

'They'll probably crash into the bollards next time instead of my window,' says Violet who is attacking the wall of her 'Infinity Blooms' florist shop with a bucket of soapy water and a brush. Her KAT is supervising from a seat in the sun, away from the splashes. Cats are like that. Self-contained as if they are allowing you the privilege of their company. This black cat was called KAT and 'owned' Violet, not the other way around. No problem remembering KAT's name. Only challenge was spelling it with a K ... Violet style.

'Have you had more problems?' I ask. 'Apart from residents mistaking the accelerator for the brake and nearly losing your front shop window.'

'No major crimes this week... Last night some idiot scrawled graffiti on my wall and took a few of my watering-cans. Must have heard about the national TV program...'

Violet knows I am anti- graffiti. I think it wastes words. Just one of my pet complaints but I usually keep it to myself. Not keen on tattoos either.

Was quite shocked when one of the F.O.B. wanted to check my arms in case I had tatts which might show FOREVER in their bridal photos. Felt like saying I had tatts in private places and none of his business, but I didn't.

Violet says, 'Sometimes it's Art, Quinn. But this graffiti wasn't. Not like my watering cans wall.'

Despite residents downsizing, this Village is full of

eccentric collections which have extended to the shopping strip outside. 'Infinity Blooms' has a watering- can collection hooked on the side wall as sculpture. The first one with painted purple petals had been a shop warming gift to Violet from an old boyfriend. The gnome watering- can with the dripping nose came later from the op shop. The dainty bone china one was rescued from the indestructible rubbish collection at the Village. The 79 others had been collected in the past year. Violet had been invited to go on the collectors' TV program but they required a minimum of 100 eccentric objects. So now she was numbering each watering- can until she reached the 100. A sort of count down to Infinite Eccentricity. She intends texting the producer sometime in the next month.

Violet scrubs at the mark. She's a stout sixty-ish but energetic with the movements of a woman a decade younger. As if she's making up for lost time.

'Does that tag look like a Z to you?'

I peer at the black scrawl. 'Maybe. Soap won't get that off. Need something stronger than elbow grease as my Gran used to say. Maybe paint over it with other artwork? Flowers? Like violets just for you? '

Violet is still examining the Z. tag. 'Why put your own name on it? Must be Zac again. Always acts before he thinks. Hoons around.'

'Flora's grandkid?'

'Yeah. A few cans missing too.' I couldn't understand why any graffiti-artist and especially an 18 year old might steal her watering- cans. Apart from nuisance value. They were just junk and most didn't even work. I wonder if it is a kind of security to have 'stuff' around you. But I'm a minimalism and Violet is a collector.

'Creates more work for me,' says Violet.

'I can see that.'

Violet shakes her head. 'Not the clean- up. 'The Wedding' people were going to feature my floristry business if I made the TV program. They're always looking for new fashion styles for flowers. Single colour blooms has been done so often,' Violet explains. 'Online bookings can help a regional shop like mine. Need a point of difference, and no-one else has a flower watering-can collection wall.'

'Probably right about that.'

'Quinn, I am the FIRST!'

I change the subject.' Violet, I noticed the yellow chrysanthemum in the bridal bouquets.'

'Yes. Vibrant. Should turn out well in the photos. No other colours at the 4 am flower market that morning.'

'Yellow means neglected love or sorrow. Just for chrysanthemums.'

Violet swore.

'Did anyone notice?'

I shake my head. 'Just me. The others thought the flowers were beautiful and they were.'

Violet said, 'Mostly I've been Googling the flower meanings to check but I did R for Roses first. Especially after a request for black roses. Haven't done C yet. So sorry. Put it off partly because of my spelling. I just call them 'mums'. '

Fabulous at floral arrangements but she can't spell which causes embarrassing moments with clients. 'Condolences' and 'Congratulations' look similar for her.

'Would you like something special written on your card with the flowers?' ensures Violet gets all the news early. Just the spelling needs help. So I hand- printed a generic list of one liner messages for her to copy the spelling. Her Valentine Day blooms with optional poems were wonderful for romantics to send. She runs the poems through Spellcheck first. Or gets me to check the wording. I've done her most- used love poem, so she just has to copy and insert the customer's name.

I've noticed that one of the reasons Violet gossips so much is that it saves her having to write things down. She prefers talking. Even talks to her plants. Claims they don't answer back. But that's ok. She puts up with all my annoying habits, so I can help a bit with the spelling.

No problem.

Violet's flowers are exceptional, not surprising she's won a few awards at the Wedding Fairs. Always love the damp earth smell when entering her shop, which is like a haven of scents. The coolness and vaguely familiar scent of roses and other bunched flowers I don't know the names of. Strange how you can 'know' and be comforted by a smell but can't put a name to it. I know 'Violet' is not her real name, she claims she started using it when she moved here from the city, so customers would remember she was the florist. That's her business, the name-change. I suspect there was another reason. She never mentions her earlier life.

'How come you knew about the yellow ones, Quinn?'

'Backpacking. I gave my French host a bunch of yellow chrysanthemums. Later I found out that any chrysanthemums are a bit of an insult to the French unless it's for funerals or All Saints Day.'

'The bride wasn't French, was she? Or her family?'

'No.'

'That's a relief.'

'Greeks call them the death flowers too.' Just thought I'd better mention it. The Pappas family told me that at their funeral.' I've done a few ceremonies for the Pappas families. Word- of- mouth recommendations are best.

In her tiny cluttered desk behind her flower-arranging high table for the long stemmed blooms, Violet Googles to check. She peers at the screen and reads out,

'White is devoted love. Red is love. The others are mainly for funerals, as symbol of immortality. Can survive in winter frost and need little care.'

'A bit like some relationships, maybe?'

Violet laughs too.

'You know I turned down that dead roses order from that divorcee who wanted to insult her ex, don't you?'

'Yes.'

As a struggling business, I admired Violet's refusal to deliver anonymous Insult Flowers. But her Apology Pot-Plants are doing well.

'Could have made a sale with yellow 'mums' instead, if I'd known what they meant then.' Violet deftly snips stems and bunches individual blooms. KAT supervises with an occasional purr.

Then Violet scatters sparkling dust outside the shop doorway.

'Like my new styling? Might deter the vandals from wrecking my watering cans, again. The dust clings to their shoes.'

'Yes it does,' I shake my shoes. Shards of light. 'And to the feet of any customers too. Might cling to Kat's fur.'

'Advertising,' says Violet quickly. 'How are your sunflowers coming on?'

After the funeral of her husband, a client had given me sunflower seeds to grow, to symbolise his life. I'm hopeless at gardening and most flowers die under my care. But in a small town I keep bumping into her and she asks me about the progress of my sunflower and requests a photo. So I bought a sunflower from Violet and photographed it with the label 'grown in the area' and didn't actually say I hadn't grown it. Violet said, 'You're a fraud. But a kind one.'

'Does the name 'Infinity Blooms' imply your flowers last longer than the couples' relationship?'

'No.'

'That the love behind the gift will bloom for ever?'

'Aw...Quinn. You are such a romantic. Not even close.'

'Is blooms a verb or a noun?'

'Quinn! Go away and write your next ceremony. Or do you just use a find-and-replace function to insert the client name? And your Albert Einstein quote?'

'Violet, that's unfair.'

I think she was joking.

Naming Day

When choosing a baby name, know that you'll inadvertently insult all those whose choice of name is NOT used. Remember future form-filling and do not include ALL relatives' names or multiple hyphens in surname. Only guarantee: the recipient of the name will hate it as a teenager or even before.

'Quinn, could you do a naming ceremony for us? The thing is, our family is a bit complicated. And now there's the new baby.'

I know Xavier from the regular Motives card game at Bea's café. I knew he had a partner with children from a former relationship, but we don't talk about family when we're playing Motives. You have to concentrate on their role in the game, not the family life of the real person who is the player. So you're talking to a genetic cyber warrior or a dinosaur using digital powers against pandemic disease. Not dad Xavier with a new baby. That's why I enjoy it. You can be someone else for an afternoon. An action super hero who is no gender. And has no kids or domestic responsibilities like painting the fence, weeding the garden or taking out the rubbish. It's my time out, and probably the same goes for the other players in the group, especially Xavier.

But recently Ella, Xavier's partner had a baby. So he was sleepless from helping with night feeds and nappy changing and couldn't afford long hours playing Motives. Fair enough. Hadn't seen him for weeks. Then he called me to book a naming ceremony.

'Ella's family is traditional. The reason we've been delaying is that each of them think we are going to name the baby after them. But you can't call a kid Anastasia Elena Katerina Sophia as well as every female form of the male family names…like Georgia, Nicola and so on. '

Xavier is a big bear-like man, with thick curly hair on his head, beard, forearms and any visible parts of his body. He's not fat, just in proportion with enormous feet and a wide handspan. In olden days he would have been considered a giant. His shoes are handmade and he always wears the same pair.

'Have you registered the birth yet?' I ask.

'No. The hospital gave us the birth registration statement for the baby. '

'That has to be done within the 60 day time limit.' I warn. Xavier shrugs. 'So I found out. People keep asking about the short-listed names we are considering. We don't have any. Or too many. It's a LONG list.'

'Oh. So what do you call the baby at home?'

'Baby.'

'As the celebrant, even though it is not legal ceremony I'll need the names for the ceremony. Given and surname.'

'Yeah. That's why I'm talking to you now. And we have to meet the 60-day deadline for the registration too. Surname we've sorted. Just mine. Lee. No hyphens. Ella agrees on that. And we'll change her kids to the Lee surname later if they wish. Otherwise it gets too complicated when we travel together. I want to have a happy family 'naming' party, not a religious ceremony, but we're both zombies from lack of sleep. Hard to find a few minutes to do anything extra.'

Sounds like it might be a difficult booking, even though the naming paperwork is usually simple. I give a certificate to formalize the happy occasion but it can't be used for ID, not like a legal birth certificate. And Xavier and Ella will need that first.

' Have you chosen some adults to promise to look after the child? They should to take part in the ceremony. A bit like godparents, but without the religion. Maybe you could look on them as mentors.'

Xavier looks uncomfortable. 'Another problem. They're all expecting to be asked. I'd prefer Un-God parents.'

'So, who have you asked?'

'No-one yet.'

For a bloke who played Motives regularly and made global choices of cosmic significance, I would have expected Xavier to be better sorted. But maybe real people were harder to organise than fictional super heroes. Especially older relatives.

'Anastasia Elena, the grandmother won't approve of a naming day by a celebrant because it's not like a ceremony in church. And then we've got the other sides of the families too.'

'Sides?'

'Ella and I are not married, well not to each other. She has two teenagers from her first marriage. And I have a son from mine.'

'Where do you want to hold the ceremony?'

'In our backyard. Come and have a look Quinn.'

At least that was decided. Xavier's place turned out to be a beautifully shaded, well maintained garden with fruit trees, vines, extensive vegetable patch, well mown lawn sloping down to a separate unit at the bottom of the hill and flowers everywhere. A bit like one of those jigsaw puzzles with lots of pink, yellow and purple flower pieces to fit in around the borders. Plus blue sky. When did he find the time to keep those flower beds? And paint the veranda of the weatherboard, rambling big house? It was a welcoming house, one of those rare ones with the right feng shui of harmonious surroundings. I'm not sure about feng shui but there are some buildings which have a welcoming air of a happy home. This has it.

'My father is a keen gardener and since he retired, he looks after the outside for us. Lives in the Granny flat down the back.' Xavier cradles a contented and almost asleep baby in his muscled arms. Xavier has more hair on his forearms than the baby does on its head.

'What's your Dad's name? '

'George.'

'Is he expecting the baby to be named after him?'

Xavier shrugs. 'They all are. Is there a limit to the number of middle names you can give a child?'

'Probably. I'll find out.'

Xavier is a bit single-focussed, the type who obsesses with things. Games are his passion. It just so happened that he is brilliant at inventing games and one of his was picked up by an international company, which means he has a big income for life. Not that you'd know that from the way he dresses in holey jeans and unmatched socks. Only his hand-made shoes are expensive, but probably because no others would fit his feet, Xavier is definitely a hidden millionaire. Money doesn't seem to register with him.

So how do I know this? My partner Art went to university with him. I knew that Xavier had invented a digital program in his early twenties that paid him squillions for life.

'Lives in another world half the time. Often walks off without paying his coffee. He genuinely forgets,' says Bea.

'Then he'll come back another time and ask me to charge him for all the forgotten bills. Picks up the tab for the others too. He's a regular customer. He's not mean, just forgetful.'

'An absent minded professor?' I suggest.

'Yes, he's absent minded but not a professor. Left school early. Just someone who got lucky with a game he invented. And the second time he got lucky was in his girlfriend Ella. She's a treasure and copes with his odd habits. The atmosphere in their house is due to her. They're genuinely happy together.'

'Maybe he got lucky again with this Baby.'

Bea nods. 'What is the baby's name?'

'Ah. That is the timely question.' I explain. 'I think it will have Xavier's surname Lee. Not sure about the rest.'

'Sounds typical of Xavier.' Bea smiles. 'He'll work it out in the end. Or Ella will.'

What could go wrong at a naming ceremony? It was only half an hour, in the garden of the couple's house. But I hadn't counted on an extended family who wanted their names to be immortalized and a grandmother matriarch who felt she was losing control of traditions. The name choice was the big issue. Or the lack of it. Maybe I could help solve that problem?

'OK, we can do the ceremony on Sunday afternoon.' We agreed on 2pm.

'Catering by Sage Café?' I query.

'Of course,' says Xavier. 'Only the best.'

I hope he remembers to pay that bill quickly for Bea's sake. Especially as he's ordered Bea's combined Mediterranean and Australian feast menu for 200 guests with dips, nibbles, salads, fruit and sweets, and side vegan, vegetarian, dairy-free and gluten- free tables of treats.

'Biggest order I've had this year,' says Bea who is thrilled.

'Have you sent out the invitations yet?' I ask Xavier.

'Ella emailed them.' He shows me.

In this case, on the invitation, the baby's name is a blank.

'I think Grandmother was expecting to be invited to a wedding, not a naming.' Xavier is competently changing the baby's nappy. That was a surprise too. 'Nappy folding is just a maths challenge' he says. 'Triangles.' The baby gurgles happily and Xavier smiles in response.

Xavier likes lists and diagrams. That gives me an idea.

Some name their babies after earlier relatives in a predictable pattern of alternate generations. George. Peter. George. Peter. Others name only after relatives who have passed away. Celebs give media-attention-getting names like North West to offspring who are afflicted for life. This baby needs a 'pleasing all relatives' name, quickly. I offer. 'This is not really my business as a celebrant. I just conduct the ceremony to name your baby. I don't choose the name. But I had an idea which might solve your problem and keep the relatives all happy. Could you give me a list of the names of all the relatives you especially don't want to offend? Their middle names too, just for insurance.'

Sleep-deprived Xavier looks puzzled. 'I'll email them Quinn. Once Baby goes to sleep.'

As I turn to leave, I remember the other question we haven't sorted.

'Who will be your supporting adults, that's the sort of non- religious or un-godparents?

Xavier looks overwhelmed. 'Forgotten about that. What do you suggest?'

'It's more what you and Ella want for your child's life. Probably best to choose a couple you can rely on. And someone to be around later if anything happens to you or Ella.' I suggest.

'Oh. That's a problem,' says Xavier as he struggles with the clips on the baby's suit. 'Supporting adults? How many? Is there an upper limit?'

I shake my head. 'Your call.'

'Motives' skills should be transferrable. In Xavier's case, maybe he needs to re-shuffle his life cards? What if I re-word the challenge as a game?

'Sort out priorities.' I suggest. 'Like a game strategy.'

'You mean like choosing super powers for characters in a game?'

'Yes. Decide on the qualities you'll need in your child's life. Maybe from people younger than you?'

'Skills?'

'Sort of. But a baby isn't a robot.'

'I know, they can't be programmed to sleep...' Xavier smiles ruefully.

Ella comes to collect the baby. Her eyes have dark shadows. Alongside giant Xavier, she is petite and fragile looking. Even hugging must be difficult for them with the size disparity. I wonder whose genes the baby will take after? 'Have you sorted the details of the ceremony Xavier? Remember you PROMISED this time.'

'Yes darling.' So Xavier organises the Naming Ceremony for Sunday in the way he would play a game, and chose his cast and titles and names.

I tried to help. Using the initials to create a new name was my idea.

I like playing with words, but getting a girl's name out of the most common initials was a challenge. Not forgetting including the name of the mother of the baby, which luckily has some repeated letters.

I check the list. Anastasia Elena Katerina Sophia as well as female forms of the male names...like Georgia, Nicola.

'You didn't include mine,' jokes Xavier looking at the card on which I've written my suggestion.

'X is the unknown. You've already contributed your DNA and a girl baby has two X chromosomes anyway.'

Xavier's red eyes widen. 'Quinn, I've always enjoyed playing Motives and other games with you, but this is an extra. Thanks mate.'

'Be diplomatic,' I caution Xavier. 'Ask Ella first. It must be Ella's choice. She will have to say that name millions of times. Start there. '

My mobile rang that night. 'Quinn, this is Ella. I just love your idea for the baby's name. Thanks for the gift of a name.'

That was a relief. Just like the royals have an heir and a spare, I had a couple of spares in reserve. GAKIE and SKUA but since the Skua was a predatory Antarctic bird a sort of brown scavenger, with unpleasant habits, not my first choice. Nor probably Ella's once she found out.

'We could make it a small cast of two 'Supporting Adults' or go BIG!' Xavier is enthused now. He emails me a list of roles. Instead of calling them Supporting Adult 1, 2, 3 he called them...the...Chorus.

I explain how I worked out the name. 'A is the most common in all your relatives names. So each will assume the A is for them. 'S' and K and I were the next most common. So if you say that this is your updated version of their traditional names, maybe all will be happy.'

ﻉﻭ

'Is this a wedding that I've been invited to?' The

grandmother sweeps up the path and past the manicured flowerbeds of Xavier's sloping backyard. 'Who are you?'

'I'm Quinn. I'm the celebrant.'

'Is Xavier getting married at last?'

'No. We're celebrating the naming of the baby of Xavier and Ella,' I explain as the couple emerge from the house, and come slowly down the veranda steps, carrying the baby, in a patchwork shawl. Behind them is a mini Xavier-look- alike: his BIG son from the first relationship. Definitely following his father's shape. Then come two teenage girls who look a bit like their petite blonde, longhaired mother Ella.

Xavier created extra roles in the ceremony for all his existing children.

They are wearing patchwork ribbons. Symbolising their past which contributes to this baby. The boy refused to wear a patchwork bow tie. He settled for multi-coloured socks which didn't match. Definitely Xavier's son. You can tell from the feet.

The music starts.

'This patchwork shawl symbolises all of you who have contributed to the creation of this new life. This baby of Ella, the mother and Xavier the father. And the brothers and sisters, cousins and grandparents.'

'Oh, are they calling the baby Anastasia after me?' the grandmother is determined to be part of this historic occasion.

'Yes. Sort of.'

'Are they calling the baby after one of us?' ask the cousins.

'Sort of.'

I can appreciate why Xavier was putting off the naming decision. This family were very definite in their demands.

'With the support of this Chorus of relatives and friends,

and with the permission of your father Xavier and mother Ella and your brothers and sisters, I name you ASKIE LEE.'

Smiling, the parents nod to their other relatives. Some look like Xavier, but none are his height and breadth. So maybe the baby daughter will not be her father's height in later life.

'In Greek drama they have a Greek Chorus...so I've put all of you in that... Supporting adults who vow to look after the child for life. The patchwork themes is to indicate all your genes which make up this baby and will influence ASKIE's future life.'

There's a murmur of surprise amongst the group and then they start clapping.

Xavier continues, 'Traditionally, the Chorus also sing, so we can turn on the music now. And maybe dance?'

Turns out grandmother Anastasia was the BEST dancer. She danced for the entire afternoon, with every relative, even her son, Xavier's father George.

Just before she left, she announced to the entire family. 'Quinn, when Xavier is ready, I'd like you to conduct his wedding. Very good celebrant, even if you're not religious like our priest.' The Grandmother swept out of the garden. 'Goodbye little ASKIE, I'm so pleased you are named after me.'

Xavier and I look at each other and smile. 'Problem solved?'

He gives me a 'Hi Five' with his giant spanned hand. My fingers look tiny alongside his.

Xavier's Theory of Unnecessary Tasks to Keep Relatives involved on day

Ring warmer, pen-tester & basket-girl of paper lovebirds to distribute. Any left-over people to be in Chorus of Support.

By Remote Control

As a celebrant, I speak at funerals, but I don't have much to do with actual dead bodies. Mine are usually in the hearse or under the wreaths.

So, being the first to find Flora's body was a shock.

There were power drop- outs in the Village during the late afternoon electrical storm. When Flora didn't reply to my promised evening phone call about the next day's wedding rehearsal, I walked to her unit with increasing concern. Flora is always punctual but maybe she also had problems with her electrical systems. Many of the Village security locking systems were affected by the power cuts but they also had manual overdrives which Claud was checking. From the roadway I could look down her grey paved drive.

There was a splash of tawny colour on the ground, behind the silver car shape which blotted out the rest of her.

'Oh no!'

I expected something to be wrong, but not this.

The double garage roller door of Unit 1/3 was jammed half way down. Flora was lying caught underneath. Head split where the door had spiked her. Arms flung out. Blood everywhere. Squashed between the roller door and bumper of her new, silver car.

Legs sprawled. One shoe off. On the driver's side, the car door was open, but the seat was vacant. The engine was running. And the ignition key was there.

'Flora! What's happened to you? 'But I'm talking to myself

and there will be no answer anyway. The street is empty, except for Flora's body on the driveway.

I can't push the door up. It's stuck pinning Flora down right across her head. Messy. Grotesque. Where's the remote? Should I reverse the car back up the drive? Or try to pull her out? Or should I call for help first? I fumble for my mobile and realize I'd left it on the re-charger. A fizzy feeling of panic is rising inside me.

Hurriedly I reach in and switch off the ignition. I can smell the heat of the engine. Not sure how long it has been running. I touch the brake. Was it on? I can't decipher the on/off symbols in this very new car. But I jerk it to the far position. That's when I realize I am panicking and could make stupid decisions. I take a deep breath.

Momentarily, I wonder if I am disturbing a crime scene.

The driveway has an incline down to the basement garage so I have to drop on my knees and twist under the front bumper bar to check Flora. I lay flat to reach her arm. I tug. I can't get her out on my own. Maybe I shouldn't drag her in case I make things worse? But if she is dead, what could be worse? Was the brake safe? Would the heavy car roll over me too? But the roller door is jammed down on her head. Where's the remote? It should be on the keyring. How can I lift the door?

I check for a pulse, vainly trying to remember last year's First Aid refresher course. Can't find a pulse. She's gone.

I know she is dead, but can't believe it.

There is no vitality left. Her face, or the part I could see from this angle, is pale and sort of empty. Contrasts with vivid bloody globs on the ground. The back of her scalp is smashed. Just a shell of the woman she had been. But her tawny scarf is tight around her throat. A bizarre splash of colour. The other end is caught by the front wheel of the car. Had the car run over her scarf, trapping her? And then the roller door came down? Which was first? Or had she been squashed by the oncoming car gaining momentum down the slope? She was the Tawny Femme Formidable no longer.

I scramble upright just as footsteps approach down the ramp.

'Is Flora all right?' asks an unfamiliar voice.

'What's happened? Oh, NO!'

And then Claud's voice. 'I've called the ambulance.'

Why would he do that when there was medical staff in the hostel? And Dr G. was down the street? But Flora was beyond first aid. Maybe Claud had to follow official procedures as the person in charge of Everest?

'Suspicious death. Roller door!' Claud says. 'Shit!'

Flora is not breathing, but I can hear my own, rasping in and out. This is what a panic attack felt like. And the feeling is getting worse.

'Dale's car isn't here. He's also got a remote which opens this double garage,' says Claud.

Residents were gathering, moving slowly down the ramps like insects in the dark. A few on walking frames. Some lived in the neighbouring units which overlooked the drive way. They stood around, uncertain what to do.

'Is it Flora?'

'Did she have a heart attack? Oh no, her head!'

'That bloody roller door again!'

'A tragic accident! Such a lovely woman.'

'Is the power back on yet?'

Someone brings out a tartan blanket. Others hover unsure what is appropriate to say or do.

Inane thoughts intrude. That unfashionable, thick tartan

blanket was not her style. She would have chosen a tawny, fluffy one. But she is gone. I can't bear to look at her so vulnerable in this way. What did fashion or style matter?

'She's passed.'

Each death brought their own closer. So there was relief mingled with sadness for the loss of Flora. Only later came the gossip and conjecture about who did what and why.

'The power was off. The remote wouldn't work. She must have been opening it manually from inside the garage. There's a manual overdrive.'

Not so simple. The car had pushed her hard against the door. Who was in the car?

'Could have happened to any of us, if the brake wasn't on properly.'

I wasn't certain about that. With a proposed change to her will, others might want her death BEFORE her marriage. Weird to be thinking of motives when Flora was lying in front of me. I kept expecting her to interrupt and say what she thought about the situation of her own death.

'How old was Flora?' asks Rocky who shares the double garage. And who also has a remote.

'83.'

'I'm 84. I'm older.' If he were older, somehow it was his kind of victory against Death. He was still alive. And the trivial comments fill in time, when you're not sure what to say. Tragic death makes all conscious of personal survival.

'She was having trouble with that roller door. A possum curled up in it a few days ago and the remote didn't work,' says Rocky leaning on his walker. 'Her new car had all kinds of devices she was trying out. I know she had trouble closing the car side windows.'

Had Flora pressed the roller door remote from inside her car?

But then she must have got out of the car to check something? The roller door was stuck part-way now. Half open or half closed? Not a possum in sight.

She couldn't drive over herself. Unless the weight of the vehicle just rolled down the drive and hit her. To do that, the brake needed to be off.

'Brake's on.' Claud checks.

'I moved it.' I admit. 'Flora had trouble with her arthritis in her hands. No strength there. '

Claud is worried. 'Ever since we opened, Flora was keen on monitoring OH&S problems. We check the roller doors regularly every month. Especially this double one. Maybe the power surge after the storm messed with the electrical system.'

Bad publicity for Everest to lose the owner in suspicious circumstances.

Claud looks up the driveway. 'I warned Flora about the gradient. We've had one crash with two motorized scooters going too fast on these ramps. But it was younger family of residents borrowing them to joy ride illegally. Not 'geriatric hoons''

Usually Claud is discreet and wouldn't use a term like 'geriatric hoons' for his clients. Shock probably.

I might be in shock too, but parts of my brain were starting to query. If the car just rolled forward on the incline, why was she facing that way? Could she have been coming OUT of the garage, rather than going into it? Maybe someone else was in the driver's seat? Maybe it WASN'T an accident?

I feel a bit shaky. Poignant to be at the sudden end of

Flora's life when she was supposed to be starting afresh with the marriage which I would no longer be celebrating.

'Where is Dale? We'll have to tell him.'

'Maybe he already knows?' says Claud looking at me and then whispers.

'They're forgetting it is a DOUBLE garage, with several having access.'

'What?'

'Rocky in Unit 3 or any of his visitors. Dale. And an over riding manual control inside. And Flora's spare key inside her front door, which visitors know about. Especially family.'

Claud whispers this to me so the other neighbours don't hear.

Ambulance and police arrive together. Then the coroner's vehicle and the forensic pathologist. I answer the official questions and leave with my own suspicions. Claud is keen on it NOT being an accident. Then I remember something I need to check with Art.

Being the first witness on the scene, I became an inadvertent sleuth in the mystery of Flora's death. Of course, the police took over the formal investigation, but as her celebrant for the intended wedding and later her memorial ceremony; I still felt an obligation to her as my client. She was still my responsibility, sort of. And I'd liked her. Especially after listening to her telling the family it was time for them to become more charitable. That took spirit.

'The security camera on the 'rocks'. Did it cover Flora's driveway too?' I ask Art who is fiddling with his programs.

'Yes it did. I angled it deliberately for maximum coverage of the double area. Even in the dark. Light sensitive to movement.' But Art's face then switches to that stubborn look when he knows he's in the wrong. He brushes his dark curl hair from his face in a nervous gesture.

'It would be timed and dated?' I ask Art.

'No luck there.'

'Why?'

'Petty theft problem within the village. Claud asked me to set up security cameras as a deterrent. One near Infinity Blooms because of the water cans missing and one near Unit 3 because of complaints about 'valuable geological specimens' being stolen. That one also overlooks Flora's drive. She requested that coverage too.'

'So?'

'He asked me to be very obvious about setting them up, as a deterrent. But they weren't actually on yet. Cost cutting.'

'Who knew that?'

'Nobody except Claud and me.'

Was Claud hushing up potential safety issues tainting the financial future of Everest, and affecting re-sale values? Or was he just trying to do his job? Then again, checking the roller doors mechanism was also part of his job.

'Did Claud know Flora intended him to oversee all her remaining properties after her death? A job for life? '

Art looks up. 'He wasn't there for the family meeting. Flora might have mentioned the possibility to him earlier?'

'If so, did he have a motive?'

'To do what? He was already managing Everest pretty well for the Body Corporate. Why would he sabotage that job?'

'True.'

These were real people who didn't act like randomly drawn Motives characters cards on a Saturday afternoon. Pity.

Art tugged my arm. 'Got something to show you. I was

updating your website with the shots we took against the rose garden at dusk.'

'Thanks,'

'And I noticed something in the background. Flora's new silver car, but Zac was driving.'

'Joy-riding again without her knowing? Could Zac have been accidentally involved in his grandmother's death? Same night.'

Art shook his head. 'No evidence of that, ...yet.'

'If you had switched on the CCTV, there might have been,'

'Piss off, Quinn.'

I escape to the kitchen to make coffee and to think. Then I return handing the steaming mug to Art as an apology. We make-up fast, usually. I can't bear us not talking.

'Sorry. The timing matters. Who might gain if she died BEFORE her wedding? Someone who gains from the existing will? One of her kids?'

'My money is on Dale,' says Art. 'Part of an elaborate scam by a con artist who had previously preyed on attention-starved, vulnerable, wealthy, older females? Were his visas genuine Quinn?'

'Still checking,' I will check. 'Considered a de facto because he was living with her...or had lived with her for the required time. Even if there was no mention of him in her will, he'd get half her assets.'

'Which will? My secret filming wouldn't count as a living will.'

'Probably not. But I witnessed some legal documents for Flora,' I confess.

'What was in them? Was one a will?'

'I didn't read them.'

'Didn't you even glance at the layout? A will's format is

pretty distinctive.' Art was exasperated.' A will can be written on a serviette and still be legal – it doesn't have to follow any legal layout. But if it was drawn up by a legal firm it would be recognisable.'

'No. I didn't notice.' Foolishly I was thinking of beetroot at the time.

'Did she lodge the original with her lawyer or would there be a copy still in the car or the house?'

'Maybe. Or perhaps Flora was just playing games with people's expectations and sitting on the paperwork?'

The caffeine in the coffee was clearing my head. Helps to talk ideas out, even if Art shoots them down. I try another angle.

'Fred's recent crash into the pharmacy, may have given someone the idea for murder set up to look like a car accident?'

Art nods and suggests, 'That brand of vehicle Flora bought, had a bit of bad coverage last week. Withdrawals because of accidents related to the pedals. And more hi tech. than she was used to. You needed to read pages of instructions first. Flora's a bit like you, only reads the manual in an emergency.'

I give a small smile. This comment is an Art overture. I do read manuals, or instructions, sometimes. Other times I learn by doing or messing up things along the way. But I also notice both of us move between past and present tense when talking of Flora now.

Art shakes his head. 'I reckon it was an accident. Something went wrong with the roller door. That's an OH&S problem for Claud. His responsibility. But if it was murder, it's not his fault.' Art was scrolling through the inside Unit 1 footage he'd taken.

'Come and have a look at this, Quinn.' Art adjusts the screen.

'Flora's front room. She's talking to her family.'

So bizarre looking at someone whom you know is already dead. Not like watching old movies with the familiar faces of long- gone famous actors playing roles. I used to do that at acting school. Here Flora looks calm, in control and just 'Flora'. I couldn't believe she wasn't around anymore. Must be comforting to believe in an afterlife where the personalities continue. I don't. Old movie clips last longer.

'Why have you kept this?'

'Flora's evidence of her intention. So they couldn't argue about it afterwards. Luckily I used batteries or the power cuts might have been a problem, although Flora's unit had electricity by then."

Art hits the PAUSE button.

'Could be murder faked as an accident. Flora was a savvy lady. And a competent driver. Maybe someone wanted it to look as though she hit the wrong pedal, and it was an accident,' suggests Art. 'Or she couldn't work the remote and got out to investigate and the car got her. Or there was a fault with the roller door.'

'Why is that relevant?

'So she'd die before her marriage when the new 'charitable' will applies.'

'And who would that be?'

'Follow the money. Take your pick. Her adult children stand to lose the most if it all goes to various charities via those trusts she was setting up. Remember what you witnessed.'

'I didn't read it. Just witnessed her signature. Would Dale know about it or have his own copy if he is a beneficiary?'

'Ask him. If the police haven't already.'

'So where's the document?'

Normally original legal documents were lodged with

lawyers, and the client kept a copy at home. So it could still be in Unit 1. Or maybe in the car? Glove box? Near the unread manual? Unless someone took it?

'But which will is valid?' I pose to Art who shrugs.

'That toxic family would need Flora to die before her wedding, then they would still inherit, rather than the charities. That is a BIG financial motive. So it would be in their interests to destroy any later will.'

But I couldn't imagine them working together. Maybe just one did it, alone. Son Ed was stupid, lazy and suffered outbursts but that didn't make him a murderer. There's a big difference between being a self-centred teenager like Zac which is fairly normal and killing your grandmother. OR being so furious about the legacy money being cut off that you feel entitled to kill as the ultimate elder abuse. Unpaid debts or even bankruptcy looming for daughters. Valid motive. But the real question was HOW? Were her children skilled enough to commit a murder? Doubtful. Difficult enough for them to organize themselves on an ordinary day, let alone plan a crime without being caught.

Manager Claud is likely to be blamed for any OH&S insurance problems.

Was the lover and con-artist Dale involved for love or money?

And what about an unknown such as Rocky next door. Opportunity as he had a key. Unlikely. No motive. Although he has a murky political past in Eastern Europe according to Violet.

As a sleuth, I'm losing the plot. Time to get some sleep.

I have an international wedding tomorrow. Acting as celebrant and after today's tragedy, I will be acting.

Lost Bride and the Pre-Nup

'Most brides are late,' I reassure Sam the bridegroom. 'And you told me Grace's family do everything at the last minute… airport check-ins, lawyer appointments…everything.'

'Not this late,' says the groom, checking his watch again. 'It'll be her step-father trying to control our wedding.'

My job as celebrant is to keep everybody calm, perform the ceremony legally and solve all problems. Tissues are part of my first-aid kit.

So are big doses of reassurance.

'The bridesmaid has already arrived and here comes the bride's car,' I pass tissues to this nervous groom to wipe the sweat. It's so hot. His increasingly sweaty face is starting to match his pink silk pocket handkerchief which is useless but fashion colour-themed by others to go with the roses. White ribbons flutter on the bonnet and tiny, perfect, pink rosebuds are visible on the dashboard as the bridal car cruises to a stop in front of the sole bridesmaid waiting on the carpet leading into the venue. But only the agitated chauffeur in his peaked cap gets out.

I peer inside. No bride. And no father-of-the-bride either. Only a discarded bouquet of pink rosebuds on the back seat which match the dashboard decorations.

'Slight problem Quinn. The bride's changed her mind. She's not getting married today.' The driver speaks very quickly fearing we'll shoot the messenger. 'The stepfather won't give her away.'

'Why?'

'Had an argument in the car. The stepfather wanted me to stop at the lawyer's office en route. She wouldn't get out of the car. And refused to sign the document. Then the stepfather had a bit of a meltdown and left.'

'So where's the bride?'

The chauffeur shrugs. 'She just got out at the next traffic lights! VERY upset. In her wedding dress! But left the flowers. And told me to drive on.'

'Maybe I can talk to her? Or suggest a compromise? Why did they argue?'

'Something about a pre-nup and the need to sign BEFORE the ceremony.'

There had been hints of this at the rehearsal a few days ago. The M.O.B. (mother of the bride) had rung several times. She approved of Sam, her prospective son-in-law, but the step -father wanted to sort the finances. Unfortunately their Hong Kong plane was delayed and they missed the rehearsal and the legal appointment.

But last-minute-witnessing-of-paperwork was not unusual when visas and overseas family were involved.

'Has Grace got a mobile with her?' I ask Lea, the rose-pink-gowned bridesmaid who is rummaging in her bag for her mobile contact list.

'Yes, down her bra.'

I speed dial. My current clients are listed. 'Grace, this is Quinn, the celebrant. Would you like me to come to you? Where are you?'

No answer. But she'll get the message, I hope.

At least today isn't New Year's Eve or St Valentine's Day

with back-to-back weddings when brides are warned that being fashionably late is NOT acceptable. A delay might be possible as it's midweek although it's high summer, a popular time for sunlit wedding photos. Maybe a postponement if the bride really doesn't want to go ahead with the wedding. That is her call. All parties have nerves on the day. Even parents.

A bridesmaid with common sense is an asset. A best man with a hangover who loses the rings is a handicap. And losing the bride now is a disaster.

I dial again.

It rings but no-one answers. Only the robotic message voice.

'This is Grace. Sorry I can't take your call. Busy getting married today. Just leave a message after the beeps.'

'Where would she go?'

'A Chinese bride in a long, lace gown, and a veil is fairly noticeable in a suburban street. Especially on her own. She'll need to change quickly,' says Lea scrolling, 'but I can't track her phone. That's off now.'

'Money?'

'Grace didn't have a handbag with her, so no purse. But she had a credit card in her bra.'

'AND her mobile in the bra?' I query. She was a tiny girl.

'We all do that if we go out for a girls' big night.' The bridesmaid nods. 'But Grace didn't plan this. Leaving the wedding car was impulsive.'

'If it's a last minute reaction, she won't have clothes stashed anywhere. Or money. Or have a ticket.'

'Grace keeps a spare set of exercise gear at the High Street gym. Or she could pay on her phone app for new clothes.'

'Any friend she'd go to for help?'

'Only me. The rest are at the wedding. Inside there.' Lea

points towards the reception rooms where the chatting of expectant guests provides a pleasant buzz which could turn into relative chaos very soon. Like tropical butterflies, female guests wear brightly coloured, sleeveless outfits with shady hats to ward off the heat. I'm wearing my neutral celebrant jacket, because it's work for me, but the heat is rising.

'Should we delay the wedding? Maybe she's trying to ring Sam? His phone will be off. Check with the best man,' I suggest. 'Whisper!'

The bridesmaid vanishes inside and returns quickly. I get the feeling she doesn't have a high opinion of the best man, who has already mislaid the rings once and is hung over. As a celebrant, I watch the body language clues.

The tight hands are always a giveaway. Lea is seriously annoyed.

'No contact yet. Best man's phone is dead. Forgot to recharge it.'

Meanwhile the best man is improvising and getting Sam more nervous. I can hear his penetrating voice in the background.

'Let's have the food first as a party and then the ceremony,' suggests the best man. 'If Grace agrees by then, we can go ahead. If not, we'll still celebrate and have a few drinks.'

The groom looks stunned, so Lea interjects.

'Everything is under control, Sam, just wait.' Willing to do anything for the bride, her best friend, except be a stand-in or marry the best man whom she obviously considers a tactless idiot with or without a hangover, Lea pulls Sam aside.

'Quinn will speak to Grace. And she'll be here in a few minutes. It's quite fashionable to be extra late. Wait in the room off to the side. It's cooler there and no-one will be watching you.'

'Okay,' says the groom who looks overwhelmed.

This wasn't an arranged marriage. They had chosen each other, but they are very young and her family is extremely wealthy in any currency. Grace is paying for the wedding, not the family, which is unusual for a Chinese family. So in my role, it doesn't matter who is paying for the wedding, the couple is always my client.

I know the prospective in-laws have insisted the Australian-born groom sign a pre-nuptial agreement before the wedding goes ahead. Grace is an international student who owns significant property that her parents have given her and she has also inherited an estate from the grandmother. Her stepfather was worried the marriage may not last, a quickie divorce might occur and the husband would take half. So he wanted a contract that, if there was a split, Grace would keep all property she took into the marriage.

'I'll get my car, and check the route,' I whisper to the bridesmaid. 'Why do you think Grace took off? The real reason?'

'It's her stepfather forcing her into signing. Grace hates noisy arguments and usually gives in. But she thinks a pre-nup suggests she doesn't trust Sam as a potential husband. Sort of an insult to him, especially as he doesn't earn much. Sam's a really lovely man. Can't say the same for his choice in mates.'

Lea glances towards the best man who is now telling the guests about the Bucks' Night he had for the groom the night before.

'Sam might feel more insulted about being left waiting at the altar,' I suggest.

Plan B. was needed. But first I had to find the missing bride.

'Would she be likely to visit an op shop to get a cheap change of clothes?'

There were several on the High Street between Grace's home and the wedding venue which was the route taken by the bridal car. And it was a weekday. Shops were open.

'Grace is not an op shop person. Vintage is not her. Can't imagine her bartering that wedding dress. Or walking home to change.'

Just then Grace's mother comes out to the car park. She's petite, fashionable and an older version of her daughter. Her outfit is Parisian designed and her shoes cost more than most weddings. We call her M.O.B. (mother of the bride) on our schedule and she's upset. Perspiration beads show underneath the perfect makeup. 'Quinn, I just want her to be happy. Go and find my daughter.'

I notice she says 'my' not 'our'.

'I'll do my best.'

I dial again. 'Grace?'

'Yes,' her voice is quavery.

'This is Quinn, the celebrant. Where are you? I'll come and help you wherever you are.'

Grace is my client, not her step-father. So her interests come first.

My old car isn't as noticeable as a cruising bridal vehicle with fluttering ribbons, so I grab my car-keys.

'Take this.' The bridesmaid gives me a bottle of chilled water. That definitely wasn't kept down her bra.

My car is much older than my mobile, so I switch on my hands –free, and keep talking as I swing out of the driveway of the function centre.

'Tell me the street name Grace. What can you see opposite?'

'A bus stop.'

'Does it have a number or a name?'

'Can't see a number.'

Less than a kilometre from Grace's home to the wedding venue. I should be able to see her soon. I track the route, in reverse. High Street is very long, but twisty, so you can't see far ahead. It's getting hotter with that summer haze of heat rising from the pavement. The street shimmers.

Even with sunglasses, my eyes ache. Then I see a small figure in the corner of the bus shelter on the opposite side of the road. A bunching of white dress collapsed on the seat. I do a U turn.

Grace!

Bus shelter 13. Bad luck. I park in the 10 minute Pick Up zone. Always an optimist.

Grace is scrunched up on the corner seat. Like a wounded bird, with veil wings of lace. Her perfume doesn't quite overpower the discarded, greasy fast food bags in the overflowing bin, dumped by previous passengers. I sit beside her and give her the bottled water, 'Lea sent this.'

Grace's eyes fill with tears. She sips.

'Just tell me how you feel…I'll listen for as long as you like…' I bring out the tissues as her eye makeup drips on the dress. Lots of snuffling.

It takes me almost the box of tissues and fifteen minutes listening as the not-yet bride and I sit in the bus shelter, with her designer dress bunched up around her tiny knees, like a toddler playing dress-ups. Two buses drive past.

Passengers peer out. She doesn't notice. But it's time to get her moving.

We can be 55 minutes late, but over an hour ruins the catering schedule.

'Would you like to speak to Sam, he's worried about you. And maybe he feels a little hurt.'

The groom was beyond worried. Grace mattered to him more than the ceremony or the embarrassment of being stood up.

'Grace...we can call it off... You don't have to sign anything...'His voice is hoarse as if he's almost crying too.

'I want to get married but I can't walk down that aisle by myself.'

'I'll be at the end of it, waiting for you,' Sam says.

'Lea will be just behind you.' A sensible girl that bridesmaid. Good in a crisis. Not just decorative and worried about how she looks in HER dress.

'But my parents?' the bride wailed. 'My step-dad has gone! He left me!'

Now was the time to mention Plan B. This bride has more than one parent.

'Sam! Pass the phone to the bridesmaid.' I instruct the groom. At this stage, I've given up on the best man. Decision time. We have to continue with the ceremony, or cancel.

'Hello. Lea speaking.'

'Quinn here. Can you get hold of Grace's mother? Say I want to ask her something privately. NOT on loud speaker phone.'

'Grace's mother? Ok I'll get her.' Lea says. 'We're in the cool room.'

Which meaning of 'cool' did Lea intend? She's a bridesmaid who chooses her words carefully and I like that.

Background noises as the mobile is transferred. I hear high heels tapping on the wooden floor.

'Hello. Yes, this is the mother of the bride.'

Glad she was still seeing herself in that M.O.B. role.

'This is Quinn, the celebrant. I've got an idea for a change of plan.'

Amazingly she agrees. The next challenge is to convince Grace.

'Anyone can walk a bride down the aisle. It doesn't have to be your stepfather. You're over 18, so you can marry.'

Meanwhile, the wedding car returns to bus stop 13 with the bridesmaid carrying a makeup bag and a first aid kit. Lea does a repair job on Grace en route. Makeup. Hair. Even sprinkles water on the pink roses in the bridal bouquet to refresh them. Rose perfume wafts.

Grace emerges from the bridal car, clutching the flowers firmly, to be met by her mother ready to walk her down the aisle. 'Are you sure you want to do this Grace?' her mother asks. 'It's your decision.'

'Yes, I want to marry Sam.'

'I'm right behind you,' Lea tweaks the dress. 'Let's go.'

'I'll sort any documents later,' says the mother as the wedding march music starts.

The guests turn in surprise and then start clapping. Mother and daughter walk arm in arm and just behind, the relieved bridesmaid holds the bridal train.

Most guests didn't realise about the bus stop detour. Being late was the norm in Grace's extended family.

Sam turns, sees his bride and smiles, 'Hello Grace. You look beautiful.' Just then, the best man drops the ring which rattles across the floor rolling in ringing circles until captured by the bridesmaid with a single lunge worthy of an Olympic athlete. Lea hands me the ring.

I start the formal part of the ceremony.

If there were an award, I'd nominate Lea for Bridesmaid

of the Year. With a commendation for quick thinking, in extreme circumstances.

A bit easier than last year's 'walking down the aisle' dispute between the biological and the step father, which I solved at the Pappas Family rehearsal by suggesting they each escorted the daughter-bride halfway. But then the biological father didn't want to let her go, for a second time. So I had to separate them, with me walking inbetween. And make it look like a customary hand-over and part of the ceremony. Celebrants need to be diplomatic but also able to move furniture to accommodate extra people walking abreast down the aisle. Or role-changing.

At the reception, Grace's stepfather apologised, blaming his tantrum on business worries, a short fuse and lack of sleep on the delayed flight and anything else he could think of. Some relatives see him as a control freak, others as a concerned father trying to provide for his step -daughter. Always best to be charitable.

Just hope he doesn't have to negotiate a divorce settlement for himself, in the near future. With or without a pre-nup agreement. Assume he has one.

Grace and Sam looked so happy after the ceremony. So was I, in the background of their photos. But relieved is probably a more appropriate word for the way I felt as the celebrant. Today I had been acting very professionally, but Flora was still on my mind.

Accidental Death?

Being still able to drive has a certain status in the village. So Flora's probable death by car was the major conversation.

Googling statistics on pedal accidents in the elderly was suddenly popular.

'Do I Google car pedal or accelerator or accident?'

'Accident is too big as a subject. Be more specific.'

They were fearful that if Flora could have an accident, so could they. In a bizarre way, they wanted it to be murder, not bad driving. The roller door accident rate didn't interest them as much, although it existed. I checked the stats. One lawyer even specialized in expensive industrial accidents and long running court cases with roller doors. Hadn't realized so much could go wrong. No wonder Claud had qualms.

Village resident-drivers were skilful but apprehensive. These were the ones who had not yet relinquished their licences. The others had been 'dobbed in' by caring family or like Fred, had been forced by repeated accidents to be retested or placed on restricted daytime or limited area driving.

Art and I were having a quick coffee in Bea's SAGE café. The smell of her daily gluten-free bread loaf experiments and hot baked rolls with unusual herbs attract even those who have no dietary issues. I eat anything. But the smell of fresh bread entices more customers every day.

The fennel and date crusty bread got us in. Even looking at the steaming crust was a sensory delight. Breaking it open. Spreading butter. Then was the pleasure of the first bite. And having a second helping. Sheer greed. I just love Bea's bready creations.

'Perfect.'

'I'm going to try 'sage' bread tomorrow,' says Bea. 'Need a signature bread or scone to go with the café name.'

'We're happy to taste samples, of anything,' Art offers with his mouth still full.

'Free Brie cheese there, for those who are not dairy-free,' says Bea. 'I'm starting to make my own cheeses. Keep them in the beer mini fridge.'

Art helps himself with enthusiasm. Earlier in our partnership, Bea called Art her brother-out-law but she's upgraded to brother-in-law. Bea has a soft spot for Art since he helped with her SAGE website for the café catering. And made a few suggestions on marketing her recipes online.

Just then, Violet drops by with the regular flowers order for the café and pauses at the outdoor tables to chat with us.

Art pulls out a chair. Violet speaks to me.

'I Googled that Isadora you mentioned, Quinn. In 1927, Isadora Duncan, the dancer, dies of a broken neck when her long scarf caught on the wheel of the car in which she was a passenger. Then I found another more recent accident.

Some bloke was found pinned between his car and a brick wall. His driveway is on an incline and his car was found still running and in neutral.

So it's happened before. Her long scarf must have got caught under the wheel. As the car moved down the incline. Maybe thought she'd put the brake on and hadn't.'

'Plus the garage roller door falling.' I add. 'That was tragically significant.'

'I don't want to think about that. Poor Flora. I prefer the

idea of the scarf and Isadora style. Better memory to keep,' says Violet. 'Not all deaths are for obvious reasons.'

'The police will look at the facts,' Art finishes his coffee.

'Maybe she didn't put the hand brake on properly? It's hard if your hands are getting stiff.'

Claud arrives and overhears.

'If the roller door is faulty, it's an O.H& S problem for me now. BUT hitting the wrong pedal or being in drive instead of reverse is extremely common. Not putting the brake on. Mistakes that can easily cause death. Once you get the stage you can't hit the correct pedal 100% of the time or know what bloody gear you're in, its time to catch the bus!' says Claud. 'Or get a half price taxi.'

'Want a calming Camomile tea, Claud?' offers Bea. 'So sorry about your Boss.'

'Yeah,' sighs Claud. 'We'll all miss her. But her death has created a lot of paperwork. The lawyers must be thrilled.'

'Chargeable months for them! 'says Art. 'Instead of chargeable minutes.'

ॐ

Dale is wearing a black tie under his white nurse jacket. A sign of respect for his former fiancée? His after- shave wafts, so his grooming routine has not been affected by the death. He's agreed to answer a few of my questions, since I found his dead wife-to-be. But only if we do it in the Everest foyer, just before he starts his next shift.

'How often did you use the double garage of Unit 1/3 to park your car?'

Dale looks a bit distracted.

'Not often. I usually came back later than Flora. Left mine in the driveway or on the street. Too difficult on the narrow driveway to turn around unless the other car was already in the garage. I prefer to reverse in, so it's easier to get out next time.'

'But you did have a remote to open the garage?'

'Of course. Flora gave it to me. But there was a spare inside the Unit 1 front door on the hook. All the family knew that. Rocky had one too. And I was stopping at a friend's place in the city for a few nights, so I didn't park at Flora's anyway.'

'Ok.'

'I was planning on being back in time for the wedding rehearsal the next day. The police have already interviewed me. I know I was a suspect initially, but it has just been an unfortunate death by misadventure. It's not a crime to 'romance' an older woman.'

'Depends on the reason.' The moment I comment, I wish I hadn't.

Dale looks me in the eye. He might have blond looks which belonged on the cover of romance novels, but... it didn't seem fair for a man to have such regular, chiselled features. 'Eye candy' didn't do him justice.

Maybe Flora was buying a living artwork for company in her last years?

Dale smooths back his hair and I wonder if he has practised this movement in his bathroom mirror. He seems so confident that he's right about all his actions and implies I'm stupid for even questioning. That makes me even more determined to continue.

'Romance?' I try to sound neutral midway between comment and question, but Dale looks up, calculating my tone. Momentarily he's unsure whether I'm dangerous or just curious. Then he decides to manipulate by pretending to confide. Fake charm obviously must work on some of his listeners but I'm atypical.

'You know I've had a few lady friends. I started out with Flora in the way I had with my previous ladies. They wanted company and an escort and were prepared to pay in various ways. Like gifts.'

'Gifts of artwork to sell on eBay? 'I ask. 'First editions?'

'Sometimes. Could be quite lucrative with the auctions. But you need evidence of provenance for artwork for that. After a while it changed. I genuinely liked her. And felt she had been 'used up' by her kids who just wanted her money and gave nothing in exchange. It seemed a bit one way. Whereas I always try to give something in return. Must be the nurse in me...'

Was he talking himself into that? Does he start to believe his own interpretations if he repeats fictions often enough? Does his fiction become fact?

'Why would I murder Flora if I'd probably be getting half after the wedding anyway?'

He had a point. Or was this just part of his charm offensive? Appearing to sound candid?

'If I was going to set up an accident it would have been after the wedding. On the cruise probably. In the swimming pool. Or falling overboard.'

'Mmm.' I'm not convinced but I want him to keep talking.

Dale glances at his watch. He is getting restless. And the charm offensive is not working on me, so he changes his technique.

'You're just the celebrant. I'm the nurse. I don't really have to answer your questions. I've already spoken to the police.'

He was the live-in lover with financial gain and I was the inadvertent sleuth.

Just depends upon your viewpoint.

What I wanted to know was whether 'murderer' was an apt label for him, or was con-artist sufficient?

Is Dale the problem? Or is Flora's death the problem?

Who? What? Where? Why? How? When?

Not that simple.

Maybe the right question is 'How much?'

Quinn's Problem Law of Q&A

Sometimes it's about knowing which is the right question to ask. Q& A is about problem-identifying not just solving a mystery. And knowing when to shut up!

It sounded as though Dale had thought about Flora's possible demise but we all had thoughts we didn't act upon. Or thoughts we did act upon which turned out to be false leads. Like the location of Flora's will.

I tend to think of boring, legal paperwork in three stages, Get it done, put it at the front door and then in my car for registered post or delivery. Occasionally make myself walk to the express post box to reach my steps for the day.

E-mail is preferable. And less walking.

Would Flora have done the same?

Had she scanned the signed document on her mobile as a record? Or could it be in her car? And it was never delivered to the lawyers for safe keeping? The will that said all her money was to go to charity after her marriage, and not to the children? Made in anticipation of marriage and therefore valid? I'd have to check with Art, the ex-lawyer. About the finer legal points.

The police have the car. No reason to allow me to look in it. But manager Claud might be permitted? He's likely to be one of her executors. And frankly he'd prefer Flora's death to be murder and no blame to him. I speed dial him.

'Hi Quinn. What is it this time?'

'Claud. Could you do me a favour?'

He contacts the police and checks. Nothing found. How disappointing. In one of those TV mysteries that would be the solution by the amateur sleuth. I'm just an inadvertent celebrant sleuth (failed).

But then Art discovers a clue on the security camera. They'd been experimenting with a test camera near the re-vamped Ever-Rest sign. It picked up Flora's car driving towards her place. Art pointed.

'That's not Flora driving. It's Zac again. Do you want to talk to him about that?'

So we did.

Confronted by Art and me and the security camera footage, a very upset Zac admits that he'd 'borrowed' his Gran's new car for the last time on the night of the family discussion. 'Just for a 10 minute joy ride around town. Trying out the headlights.'

'Key?' asks Art.

'Everybody knew Gran kept her spare car keys and remote on the hook just inside the front door. I 'borrowed' them on the way out after her talk about the charities. Thought I'd probably never have another chance to drive it again if she was going to live on a cruise ship for the rest of her life.' Zac blinks and his voice is quavery.

For once Zac is showing a little emotion about losing his grandmother. Blinking a lot. He looks a bit watery around the eyes.

She'd been the only strict one in his family. And maybe he was beginning to realize it was caring not just control when she placed limits, even if he broke them. Or maybe he was having to face the consequences of his actions for once. His

Gran had gone, permanently. And maybe he had contributed to that loss.

I was starting to suspect Zac of serious crime until he offered his own theory on his grandmother's death.

Zac says, 'Like…I was only driving for a few minutes. When I got back with the car, the remote wouldn't work. Like…no lights anywhere, apart from the car headlights as I drove in. Just left the car in the drive. …Cool to drive that with all the new controls.

Thought I'd put the brake on ok. Didn't know anything happened to Gran. She must have come out of the unit like… through the inside garage door. And tried to open it. And the car rolled down by itself, but after I left.

'So why was the driver's door left open? Maybe Flora got in the car after you left?'

Zac looks thoughtful. 'Gran had this big shoulder bag. When she hoisted it on her shoulder, sometimes that knocked against the keys. Hit the remote, the car opens and the lights go on. I'll give you a demo. With your keys Quinn.' Zac grabs my shoulder bag.

'No point. My car is too old. It doesn't have remote locking.'

'Oh.'

Art shakes his head. 'That only unlocks the car. And lights flash. It doesn't open the car door wide. There was a key in the ignition. And anyway, Flora was inside the garage. And there were intermittent power failures that day.'

'Ok, there's a fact which will back up my story.' Zac offers this in a desperate tone. His voice is quavery again but I can't tell whether this is due to fear, belated voice breaking at 18 or fondness for his grandmother.

'Which is?' Art looks so short alongside the head taller Zac in the green hoodie.

'I'm on the other web cam facing the rocks and Gran's drive. I'm the one in the hoodie.'

'That camera wasn't on.' Art looks up into Zac's eyes.

'Really?' Zac looks relieved and then aghast.

'Cos I left in such a hurry, maybe the driver's door didn't close properly. Later I heard Claud saying he was worried 'cos the roller doors hadn't been checked last month. His 'sort-of-mistake'. Might have been part of the accident. Ed says so. He had trouble with the roller door too. Like…So maybe it wasn't all my fault. But I'll miss Gran.'

He looks teary. 'Got to go!'

'Art, what do you really think about Zac's story?' I ask after Zac decides to leave. 'We were pretty confronting in our questions to an 18 year old.'

'He's got to face reality. But I don't know how we could prove his story. Someone left keys in the ignition and left the door open when they got out in a hurry.'

'Zac seems genuinely upset.'

'We all are. Isn't that why you're trying to solve what really happened?'

'You don't think he left his own grandmother lying on the ground with her head split open!' I say.

'Maybe he didn't see her,' says Art. 'He did mention Ed having trouble with the roller door too. But doesn't say when.'

'What do you think of this?' I offer my theory.

'Zac returns the car to the driveway, thinking she was out. Flora had been inside, checking on that elusive possum. Maybe trying to use the manual overdrive, as the remote wouldn't work after the power failure. Heard a car being parked and came out to see whether it was Dale, Claud or her car. It was dark. Maybe she hadn't even noticed Zac had taken the car or her keys. Especially if she didn't go outside, but entered from the unit's internal door to the garage.'

Art listens attentively. He nods but I don't think he's buying this version. I keep going.

'Panicking, Zac did a runner, leaving the keys in the car, but not securing the brake.

Unaware that the car rolled down moments later and squashed his grandmother against the door.'

Watching Art's face, I know he is not convinced. But I keep going.

'Knew about the security web cam on the 'rocks', and expected to be recorded, despite his hoodie covering his face.

Later heard Claud saying the cameras were not on.

Stricken with guilt but not wanting to confess. Thought that Dale would be blamed. Or death by misadventure (even if he didn't know that legal term). Contrite about the accident to his grandmother but still unwilling to accept responsibility.'

I've almost convinced myself.

'Quinn, maybe you're right' says Art. 'But it's too late. I hope Zac learns to face up to what he's done or NOT done. Legal charges are another matter.'

ॐ

Zac is pouring paint from the watering can, onto his artistic composition, on the ground in front of Unit 1. He looks pale as if he hasn't slept.

'Is that a face you're making?' I ask. 'That's one of Violet's watering cans, from her wall sculpture.'

'I recycled it,' says Zac. 'Have one for each colour. The painting is of Flora, my Gran. Abstract, like she used to do at her painting class.'

A tribute? Zac's painting was an acquired taste. Not mine.

'When I went down to the garage to get my car fixed, I saw the spray painters. Like gave me an idea. Gran had quite a few valuable paintings and Dale was flogging them on E-bay'

'So?'

'Thought I might become an artist, now that Gran's not leaving me any money. Like flog them on E-bay.'

Good luck with that. But maybe Zac had a few of Flora's genes, somewhere. The Body Corporate wouldn't be too keen on this 'art' messing up the uniformity of the residents' units.

'Violet might like her watering cans recycled back to her,' I suggest to Zac.' She needs 100 for the TV program.'

'Whatever.'

No fast change in attitude there. Still Zac-centric. But he was mourning his grandmother in his own way.

And a little later I notice Zac hanging around 'Infinity Blooms' wall. KAT was rubbing against his legs, purring. Cats pick up on human feelings, especially sadness. And the 'borrowed' watering cans were back in place on the wall, or I think they were because Violet was looking happier. And a few seemed to have extra paint splashes but hard to tell amongst almost 100 of them.

❦

In the cool, recently watered haven of the florist shop, Violet shows me her latest poem. Damp bunches of violets are grouped artistically in tiny vases on the counter. I'm thinking of including more poetry in my wedding ceremonies and on the order- of- ceremony brochures. I'd like to credit Violet as the poet too.

'Most romantics would like that.' I hand the love poem back to her.

Violet looks up. 'But...?'

'There's sex, gender and romance. And within those, people can have different preferences.'

'But...?'

'This poem has pronouns which suggest only a male/female relationship. A hetero-romantic is attracted to the opposite sex. And that's the audience most love poetry is written for. Like this.'

'So...? Who have I offended this time? Which label did I get wrong?'

'For example, I'm asexual but I'm also a romantic. '

'What does that mean?' asked Violet. 'You know spelling is a problem for me.'

I try to explain.

'Asexuals can fall in love like anyone else, they just don't want sex. Not interested in physical sex. Don't feel a physical attraction for the other person. Male or female. That's me.'

'How does Art feel about that? Seven years together without sex? Do you sleep together?'

'Yes, and....'

Violet shakes her head. She blushes.

'Aw...you don't have to answer that. Quinn. Too personal. Too much information.'

I shrug. 'All relationships are different. We negotiate. We care about each other. We have feelings for each other. We just don't have intercourse. We share other interests. We're a couple.'

'Is Art asexual too?'

'No.'

Violet looks closely at me. Having someone's 100% attention is unusual.

'So how does that work? Does he have other sexual

partners?' Or does he pleasure himself? Or does he have a low libido?'

This is one of the moments when I have a chance to explain. But I'm not sure how to tackle it. 'Infinity Blooms' is the gossip centre of town. Telling Violet could mean telling the world. But was it an opportunity to change attitudes? Or was it being disloyal to Art? He recently asked how I'd feel about an additional 'just sex' relationship for him with a female friend. Would I permit it with someone we know? Not like the sharing we have. Just a physical extra.

Violet nods as if she understands my dilemma. I wonder about her sexual history before she moved to this country town. Maybe some angst in her earlier life? She's always been quiet about her past. As if a few years have been missing somewhere.

But that's her business.

'A specific someone?'

'Mmm.' I don't want to admit I don't know yet.

'How does she feel about that?' Violet asks me. 'The female friend?'

'We're in the trial stages. Just discussing the idea. I'm happy to accommodate whatever he prefers or needs.'

'Have you met her yet? Do you already know her?' asks Violet.

The alarm bells begin in my head. This is NOT a good idea to share.

'Just keep it to yourself Violet.'

Violet confesses, 'Currently I don't have a partner. KAT doesn't count. Since my marriage ended, I decided to re-invent myself. Be a different personality. But I'm still a romantic. And love to hear about other happy relationships.'

Violet hadn't mentioned her marriage ending before. Was that when she'd changed her name?

'I am a romantic too. Probably couldn't be a celebrant if I weren't. Same for you as a florist because you're helping people acknowledge emotional times with flowers. Then there's the variation of whether you are interested in a similar gender.'

Violet shrugs and sorts her poems into piles.

'It's so hard to use the right words without offending someone. And if a label like queer belongs to your group, are you the only one entitled to use it? Makes life difficult for the rest of us. Too many difficult words to spell.'

'There's always Dr Google.'

Violet smiles. 'Do you get crushes or other romantic feelings for people of any gender or are you entirely about friendship, ice cream and mysteries?'

'Art and I love each other, in our own way.'

'I'm relieved about that.'

'But we disagree sometimes on whether to 'pass' as 'normal' around here.'

'You mean in here? With me?' Violet glances around the perfume-laden shop. Flower arrangements in portable vases crowd the floor space too. Greeting cards and chocolates for last minute gifts fill the shelves near the counter. Customers buy more than flowers from a florist.

I shake my head. 'No! Outside in the world Art's parents live in.'

'Oh.' Violet starts to wrap a bunch of tulips in paper matching their deep yellow. 'Lots of customers tell me their stories. Everybody thinks they are different. But some are more different than others.'

'Is that a quote?'

Violet says, 'No I made it up.' She shrugs. 'I don't read much.'

I try to explain.

'Art thinks we shouldn't have to hide a huge part of our identity so we don't get criticised or attacked. That's why he picks up gender issues on his programs sometimes. His parents don't approve of us living together.'

We smile sort-of comfortable with each other.

Violet looks at me. 'Sometimes you say what I feel and don't have the words or spelling to use.'

'Wow! We're getting a bit serious here.'

'You're just Quinn as far as I'm concerned. Can you fix up my spelling on this poem please?

'Sure,'

So I do. And ask her if I can use it in my next wedding ceremony, with a credit to her.

'To Infinity Blooms please.' requests Violet, 'That's going to be my poetry name. Good for the flower advertising too. Art suggested it for my website.'

Rarely would I be booked to perform a wedding and a funeral in the same month, for the same client. Initially, the police and Coroner were waiting on the post mortem report before the body could be released. Most suspicious deaths had a post mortem. Not always but mostly. The Coroner asks the senior next of kin if they have any religious or other objection – and sometimes they do – the Coroner will then make a decision. Ed was the senior next-of-kin and had to make his mind up.

Difficult.

Apparently Flora had sent her latest will with special clauses in anticipation of her marriage, to her lawyer by e-mail, scanned on her IPhone and by snail mail as a backup. Art gave a copy of his recording to the police.

So we were in a legal limbo.

Then the funeral arranger contacted me.

'The family would like to hold a memorial ceremony instead of a funeral.

That ceremony can happen immediately. The funeral will be at a later date to be determined.'

I had already been paid for the wedding so the family decided they'd convert the celebrancy deposit to a memorial ceremony. They were becoming a little more conscious of bills and who might have to pay them. For Flora, I would have done any ceremony for free. I wanted her to have an appropriate send -off and memorial, regardless of what the police or courts decided later. Or if there was a long running insurance case, keeping lawyers employed forever with chargeable minutes, days and weeks.

On her trike-bike with the flower basket-trailer, Violet makes a special delivery of black blooms as her private memorial for Flora.

'Black?'

'Daughter No 1 said mourning flowers would be appreciated. And she is Zac's mum. He's been hanging around 'Infinity Blooms' trying to be useful. I think he's got his eye on riding my trike bike, but that's not happening for a while.'

'Morning flowers. The ceremony is in the morning. I didn't think black flowers existed.'

'We are called Infinity Blooms. Can deal with infinite requests.'

'Eh.'

'I used white blooms. Took me ages to soak the stems in

a black solution. It slowly goes up the stem. Too slowly. So I sprayed them black too.'

The roses were unlike any I'd seen before.

'Memorable.' Ambiguous but useful.

'You start with white blooms and either spray or soak stems in a dye solution.'

'Are they symbolic of death?'

'No, just being fashionable. Black is the favourite colour for weddings now. Maybe I can enter them for The Wedding special?'

Despite various suspicions, the official conclusion was that it was an accident, not a suspicious death. Death by Misadventure.

Zac was cautioned about leaving the scene with possibly the brake not fully on and about his 'joyriding'. Given a number of hours of community service to perform.

Looks like she was coming out of the garage when the roller door fell on Flora. Then the car rolled on the drive and pressed her against the door.

Or vice versa?

'The other possibility is she didn't put the brake on properly because of her arthritic hands, and it just rolled over her.'

Why were the security cams not on?

'My idea,' says Claud. 'Not Flora's. It was one way of reducing Rocky's complaints. And strictly speaking 'Infinity Blooms' was outside the Village and not our Body Corporate responsibility. Although some of the shops are leased from another of Flora's companies.'

❧

With their mother gone, this family was rewriting their history. There was nobody left to blame. Now they had to organise themselves.

'Dale was just an employee,'says Daughter No 1. 'Flora was his Boss and now we are. And I was my mother's favourite.'

Maybe she needed to think that. It's not always about the amount of money; sometimes it's about favouritism. Who did the parent love more?

'The Psychic' is here to arrange Flora's memorial ceremony!' explains Daughter No. 2. into her mobile. And took a 'selfie' of us with her in the new black fashionable outfit she'd tried to put on her mother's account but discovered the credit cards were frozen.

'Celebrant,' I correct. 'I'm not a Psychic.'

'Whatever. Are you celibate? Is that what you said?' asks Daughter No.1.

'No. I'm a celebrant. I'm here to celebrate the life of Flora.'

Flora's children came to the conclusion that if she died BEFORE she re-married, they'd inherit. After the wedding, it could go to Dale, her new husband, unless she deliberately added a separate clause. They were furious when they discovered she had. AND the charity bequests still stood.

When yelled at by the offspring, Dale spoke quietly and with dignity. 'I was genuinely fond of Flora. And I've decided to make over my share to a project we discussed. Co-aged Living Charity. Age is relative. Common interest matters more.'

'Sex,' mutters Ed.

'Important that we mix with other generations and not cast type a person by their age. Flora was keen on Co-Aged a social project from the Netherlands, where university students shared accommodation with older residents, rent- free but only if willing to eat and share tasks. Results indicate more respect and less ignorance about the others lives, regardless of age…more emphasis on common interests.'

This sounded like paraphrasing a political advertisement for aged care. I think Dale was for real in public, but still not 100% sure. Also heard he had a new lady, in private, with a big art collection which had all the legal provenance necessary before selling on EBay auctions.

I prepared my eulogy for Flora. At least I could pay her tribute in this way as unlikely any of her children would be the eulogist. I'm always wary of offering a chance for open microphone tributes, as once they start; others follow in the same vein. And the ceremony goes well over the hour which I consider the absolute time limit.

Or the person you least want up there –gets up to speak and starts ranting completely inappropriate stuff – like I think this family would –… Flora loved me more – I'm here to contest the will…'

Beyond 60 minutes and you start hearing snores from older people in the audience.

We avoid that.

Dale walks up to the microphone. 'I haven't known Flora as long as other family and friends, but…'

Murmurs from the listeners. But he speaks well and pays tribute to the Tawny Femme Formidable although he didn't use the term. That's just my private tribute to her.

Flora wasn't a fool. She did have a few suspicions about Dale's intentions, as he had inherited significantly from previous relationships to older women. But she thought his attention was worth the risk. And maybe she was right.

I suspect Flora did not intend to disinherit her children. She just wanted to shock them as a temporary measure and get them under control for the wedding at least. That's why she didn't use her lawyers. That's why she used Art and me.

'The lawyers say that Flora added an extra clause to her current will. If she died in suspicious circumstances, her charitable legacy plan is to continue and prospective husband Dale is not to inherit. Zac is to inherit her car when he is 30 if he has no further convictions.'

So she was more savvy than many thought. I remember the Tawny Femme Formidable with respect.

And Zac has started hanging out at 'Infinity Blooms', helping Violet as it's walking distance from home, and he has no car, yet.

I had another funeral on Monday afternoon. Mrs Prudence Smith-Jones-Taylor-Chang-Katz.

I have to read this out as part of the ceremony. Not happy about that. The deceased client decreed it in her instructions, along with a tight script for the whole ceremony, including her self written eulogy which goes for 60 minutes. No reminiscences from friends, because there did not appear to be any. Only a small attendance with her financial advisor, lawyer, husband and a few residents who enjoy afternoon teas with fluffy scones, raspberry jam and clotted cream provided by this funeral home.

'To my husband. If he remarries to any of the Residents, I'll come back and haunt them in the bedroom. I'm even watching over this funeral.'

RING RING RING.

At that moment, someone's mobile goes off.

The ex-husband quakes. And so does his lady friend sitting alongside.

I keep a straight face. A celebrant must always put their client first. And unsure if that instruction came from above or below.

Quinn's Grave Theory: Ignore Grave threats of Everlasting Revenge by an Ex-spouse. Haunting penalties are difficult to administer in chargeable minutes AFTER a funeral.

The Almost Buddhist Wedding

'Another dead goldfish floating in the tank,' says Zac.

Alongside the larger potted plants of 'Infinity Blooms', Violet has goldfish in a well-maintained tank but loses a few fish, as most of us do. Zac scored the job of getting rid of it and flushed the dead fish down the toilet.

'Do fish have a religion?' asks Zac. Clumsily, he carries a bucket of damp ferns through Violet's florist shop just missing a waist -high, lime- green, ceramic frog. His wet footprints leave a Big Foot trail and I wonder if the mess and breakages he creates, is even more costly than casual rates, since he's been helping out. Zac has adopted Violet as his elder woman guru, which she quite likes although she's still wary of loaning him her adult bike trike for deliveries. 'Do plants…?'

'Do plants what?' Violet is arranging blooms, so they blend from delicate lemon, through vibrant yellow to deep gold and bronze. Like a temporary floral tapestry but with the bonus of wafting perfume.

'Have a religion?' persists Zac. 'Like…go to heaven or whatever …holy- sort- of- place when they die?'

'Plants become mulch. Or fertiliser. Ask Dr Google about goldfish. Some people believe in re…that longer re-cycling word, but our goldfish was a goner. And it wasn't KAT's fault this time.'

'I called it Goldie, the goldfish,' says Zac defensively 'You talk to plants, I can give the dead goldfish a name.'

KAT watches from a comfortable spot in the sun. I suspect supercilious cats who look as though they are superior to humans. KAT is definitely in that category. I suspect some earlier missing goldfish were probably not flushed down the municipal plumbing. Nor buried out the back of the shop. Obviously I'm not a cat person. I prefer clumsy humans, even of the Zac-centric adolescent variety. Easier to work out their motives.

Violet is bunching daffodils and jonquils in rustic buckets in her footpath display outside 'Infinity Blooms'. I am on my way to a coffee at Bea's café as a family catch-up but really to try her latest bakery experiments. The mixed floral and earthy damp fern scents waft as I pass. I attend so many funerals with wreaths that it's wonderful to visit this shop and just enjoy the flowers. I buy a bunch and Violet wraps them skilfully in golden paper with the Infinity Blooms sticker as Zac hangs around.

I suspect Zac is thinking about his Gran's death.

'Some religions believe in the spirit recycling. Re-incarnation. You come back in another form, according to how well you lived in your present life.' I don't believe in that, but some do.

'Even goldfish?' Zac shrugs. 'Get real. I don't think I was a goldfish before. Or a cat!'

'Up or down the scale,' says Violet. 'My friend Serena believes in that re-stuff. She's a sort of almost Buddhist.'

'Really?'

'Not like my male client with the standing fortnightly order for a dozen long stemmed red roses for 'My Darling, with my everlasting love.'

'How romantic,' I say, but Violet shrugs.

'It's a multiple order to five different women. I do believe Karma will catch up with him one day in a town this size.'

'Who's Karma?' asks Zac overhearing.

'How many watering cans now, Violet?' I change the subject.

'Ninety- nine,' interrupts Zac. 'She made me count them.'

The possibility of the TV eccentric collectors program filming her 100 watering cans has enthused Violet to update her shopfront daily. Today is a riot of yellow. Earlier it had been fairy sparkle dust leading into the shop. She records the displays on her phone. Zac had become involved via the court order of 20 hours community service. Through 'Infinity Blooms' contacts, Violet had found him community projects to fulfill his required hours. Now Violet gets him to do the 'grunt work' for her eccentric décor or take photos. He complains but Zac found he likes working with his hands. And she pays him casual rates now. He likes the money.

'That Zac is full of questions,' says Violet. 'But before you have your coffee, I've got one for you Quinn. Can a celebrant marry a couple, without the new husband seeing all the new wife's earlier documents?'

'Why?'

'So he can't see how many times she'd been married before. And her real age. I've got that friend who is a bit embarrassed about how many marriages she's had already. Serena doesn't want to scare off her new fiancé. She's concerned that he'll be worried by her short attention span with men. And that she's been a bit fanciful with the truth at times… nothing serious just a few cosmetic changes with dates…She has made bad choices in the past, but in my opinion, the new man Ged seems okay. You know him, the local supermarket manager. Art interviewed him a little while ago on Channel Zero.'

I remember Ged. Hardworking. Decent. Respected by his staff. Still single in late middle age. Usually means baggage of some kind. 'Are there any religious or legal complications with this match? For him?' I ask.

'I'm not sure. She changes her religion as often as she changes her males. Serena has offered to be my meditation tutor. She says I need to calm down. Does a fantastic job teaching primary kids to meditate. Not sure if any kind of flowers are appropriate for a Buddhist wedding. Do you know?'

'I think it is mainly prayer flags and white scarves.'

'I'll have to find out. If it goes ahead. There's a bit of a temporary problem about the Happy Buddha Enlightened Beer brand. That protest down at the supermarket. Ged's supermarket stocks the beer.'

'Is that a problem?'

'Serena's friend Maddy wrote that protest letter about insulting religious values by selling the Buddha shaped beer.'

'Mmm.' Could be a difficult wedding ceremony if the friend was feuding with the groom and ruining his business.

'I don't think Buddhist ceremonies have bridesmaids. But if Serena has one, will it be Maddy?'

'Yes.'

That could be challenging.

'I'll ask Dr Google about the Buddhist flowers,' grins Zac as he trails more wet footprints into the shop and drops a bucket of ferns near the step. KAT moves to avoid the splashes.

I explain that I have to see the paperwork a month before the wedding so I can fill in the Intent of Marriage. And after the wedding, they each get copies of the official Marriage

Certificate, which has dates and ages on it. So the truth will be visible. Unless someone has committed perjury and written lies.

The couple must complete their notice of intent with both parties knowing what is included on that form – and it must be lodged a month before, because it's about identity. One of the grounds on which a person can challenge a marriage is based on identity.

'Tell Serena to ring me and we'll make an appointment. Got to go. Bea is expecting me. I'm her official taste-tester today.'

My sister has been experimenting again. Cinnamon buns. Sweet potato bread. Herb rolls. SAGE baking is quite experimental. Bea rarely has the same items on the chalked menu outside. And she can spell, and has legible printing, unlike Violet.

'For you,' I hand my sister the bunch of flowers Violet wrapped. 'My motive is bribery. So I can taste your new rolls for brunch…are they sage flavour as promised?'

'Greed. A predictable motive,' says Bea, smiling at the flowers. She usually beats me at our Motives card games. Unless I can persuade her to play as my partner like at the Tournament weekends.

'You know I have a regular order with Violet but flowers are always welcome. Yes, I'm still trying for a signature roll. What do you think of these?' Bea slides a tray of still warm rolls onto the counter. She separates them and puts one on a plate for me with a generous pat of butter.

The aroma of new bread is wonderful. I take a bite of the brown roll.

It looks 'healthy'. But the sage flavour is awful. Should a

taste-tester who is also a relative and wants to live a bit longer, be honest?

'Er, a work in progress, I think. Prefer last week's date ones. Or the bacon ones. Any coffee Bea?'

౭๖

'I need evidence of date and place of birth, and photo ID and evidence of the end of the previous marriage for each of you,' I explain to the couple as we meet out back in the supermarket office. I usually go to a client's home but Ged's workplace is easier as he's on High Street. His 'Super-on-High' supermarket office is crammed with crates and boxes. And a bottle of Happy Buddha Enlightened Beer is in a rotund green bottle on his desk anchoring a letter. But he pulls out a couple of chairs for us.

'No problem,' Ged hands me his documents. 'I haven't been married before. I'm 55.'

'These are my documents,' Serena gives them directly to me.

Checking Serena's documents, I discover her real name is Jane Smith. Seems like she's re-invented herself a few times. Even more interesting, I discover a serial wedding person. But the four marriages were all legal.

'Do you have your divorce papers?'

Serena nods and glances sideways at Ged who seems engrossed in finding his credit card in his antique wallet bulging with receipts and miscellaneous papers. Not sure whether he's being tactful about his fiancée's papers or his filing system is non-existent. Since he has managed the local supermarket deliveries and stacking for years, maybe he's just giving her space?

I check Serena's details. She only needed to give me

evidence of the termination of the last marriage, but Serena tells me there have been four. The dates are accurate on paper, but maybe Serena gives her version elsewhere. Not uncommon, but I wonder if Ged is taking a gamble on the length of their married future. I'm always optimistic about romance. Others call it naivety.

Serena is a sweet-faced fifty-ish, and it is possible to see the 'cute little girl' behind the fading blonde curls and desire to have a sense of purpose.

According to Violet's local gossip, the teachers like the students learning Serena's techniques for calming down. Part of the comparative religion program.

In our country town, some businesses are closing, and with growing unemployment, even food shopping is affected. Keeping his existing supermarket customers matters for Ged. Having a silent protest with a religious connection at the front of his store is an embarrassment. And bad for business.

'I'd like a Buddhist- styled wedding ceremony,' says Serena. 'I've done Catholic, converted to Orthodox, then Islam and last year I was a Quaker. I simplified my life with the Society of Friends and de-cluttered.' I'm a bit surprised at this fast history of spirituality but Ged who is built like a stocky farmer with muscled arms, just looks proudly at his bride-to-be.

'Religion isn't a fashion style.' I caution, but ultimately the client's wishes prevail. Sounds like dilettante Serena has been shopping at a religious supermarket but that's not a diplomatic comment to make considering where we are. And acquiring another husband isn't exactly de-cluttering.

'Have you considered a Buddhist monk to conduct your ceremony?'

'No,' says Serena.

'Have you thought about being married in a Buddhist monastery?'

'No. Too complicated. So many different kinds of Buddhism.'

'Which kind are you?'

'I'm an Almost Buddhist,' explains Serena who has a beautiful smile and a calm manner.

'Er, what does that mean?'

'I'm interested in meditation. Only the breathing and mindfulness. And I've read the Dalai Lama.'

Not exactly what I meant. I was thinking more of Tibetan, Zen or Japanese spirituality which have complex philosophies.

'Were you brought up Buddhist?'

'No.'

Most religions prefer their followers to be married or farewelled within their own churches, temples, Tibetan gompas or chapels. So the clients who come to me are often from mixed relationships, with visa complications, family baggage as it's second time around, or have very fixed views. Sometimes they're just in a hurry to get the legal stuff over or want no fuss. Occasionally their parents need to be appeased by a nod towards their traditions. But each person must be giving real consent to marry.

Personally I'm Agnostic, and open minded about spiritual or divine beings. Still waiting on proof. If clients want me to include their wedding customs or funeral traditions, I always oblige.

'I'd like to have a Buddhist styled wedding,' Serena repeats. 'With an exchange of blessings and the white scarves.'

'Any complications with the 'Ban Buddhist Beer in Supermarket' sign out the front?' I ask. 'Strictly speaking, it isn't a 'Buddhist beer', it's the label and bottle shape.'

'That's my friend Maddy. Protesting against Happy Buddha Enlightened Beer'. Serena points to the sample green bottle on the desk. 'She wrote that letter of complaint.'

Despite Buddhist weddings not usually having bridesmaids, self-appointed bridesmaid (and serial protester) Maddy has organized a boycott of Ged's local supermarket. She wrote, 'The local supermarket is stocking a brand of beer called "Happy Buddha Enlightened Beer." As a new Buddhist, I find this 'branding' offensive to Buddhist society as a whole. The satirical use of our religious leader offends the whole religion which is widespread throughout the Asian-Pacific region. As a Buddhist we practice loving kindness, and I am asking for nothing more than fundamental respect for all, whether they be a Buddhist themselves or are merely witness to the viciousness of this particular reference. We want this product removed from supermarket shelves.'

'Take Buddha off your shelves!' was the slogan on posters.

Until now it had been a silent protest outside our Super-on-High supermarket. Confused customers had to push their shopping trolleys past silent Maddy holding a sign with a picture of the beer brand and a cross over it. Banners with the boycotted product were behind her head.

'Is it religious intolerance? Spiritual abuse?' Shoppers pass by uncertain whether she is for or against Buddhism or anti-beer drinking. Or anti-supermarkets and in favour of weekend community markets.

'Just another day at the office,' Ged jokes. 'But I'm waiting on the response from my headquarters.' Easy-going Ged seems to prefer others to make his significant decisions. And Serena looks caught between the priorities of her friend and potential husband.

But then, while we're chatting about wedding details in

the back office, the violence erupts! Shouts. Threats. Carloads of footy hoons, fuelled by an afternoon's drinking arrive. They wrestle the sign from Maddy, pushing her aside. There is a crack! The supermarket window shatters. The hoons help themselves to bottles from the crates inside the supermarket liquor counter. They open a few.

Green bottles are hurled. One hits Maddy on the head.

By the time we get to the front of the supermarket, Maddy is on the ground, crying with rage.

'I can't understand some people. Why throw the beer bottles at ME! I'm in favour of taking them off the shelves.' says Maddy. 'I'm protecting the spirituality of Buddha. Mine is a peaceful protest.'

'This was a booze fuelled attack,' says Ged grimly helping her up. 'Nothing to do with spirituality. Or religion. Just thugs! Pointless destruction. Vandalism. I recognize a few of those faces. But a few bully-boys have been imported from outside too, just to make trouble.'

Luckily Ged's staff had done first-aid courses. They patch up Maddy.

Looking tearful, Serena has an arm round her friend. Ged tidies up and puts protection across the broken window. 'I've got the glass bloke's number on my phone.' He rings the emergency glass replacement company.

'Let's have your Buddhist themed wedding, Serena' says Ged. 'I'll make up my mind about whether to continue selling the beer later. Hoons smashing my window are not going to bully me. Especially if bully boys have been imported from outside. It's not about respect for religious freedom, it's about power. '

I'm surprised by Ged's stand. And beginning to admire the man.

❧

Buddhism is a peaceful religion. The comparative religions course in the primary school was a nod towards the town's newcomers of different faiths. That's why volunteer Serena was allowed to teach her version of Buddhist meditation.

When Ged's store originally advertised 'Happy Buddha Enlightened Beer' there was a complaint that the Buddha 'branding' was spiritually offensive.

Country towns attract temporary protesters like Maddy who get 'outraged' by issues while often the locals get along quite amicably.

Serena is also a newcomer to the area. 'I'm a volunteer at the primary school. I teach Buddhist meditation. The beer was nothing to do with me. I don't even drink beer.'

'Beer isn't food. It's not a necessity of life.'

'Not sure about that,' claims the footballers.

Big media kerfuffle on a slow news day in a small town. Art did a few interviews on Channel Zero.

'Keep the bottle, toss the beer,' was caterer Bea's advice after taste-testing 'Happy Buddha Enlightened Beer'. 'I'm not getting the Nirvana supposedly found in this beverage.'

I agree.

I'm not an expert on religions either. I've got a working knowledge of the differences. Hinduism. Buddhism. Islam. Only find out details of customs of the minor ones if I have a client. Generally they tell me what they want and why. Often they've left their traditional religion or didn't know much about it but want to pay tribute to their elders beliefs. I show respect for spiritual symbols like crosses that are significant to others. I try NOT to offend unintentionally. So easy to get things wrong, so I usually read up on colours, like the

Buddhist flags. I knew green was related to nature but didn't understand why a green bottle might cause trouble. But probably it was more the commercial crassness of suggesting enlightenment if you drank this beer. And the Buddha shape and name.

A civil celebrant isn't permitted to conduct a religious ceremony, but we can incorporate cultural elements.

Meanwhile, back to the legal wedding preparation.

'Serena and I would like YOU to marry us. We've decided.'

'What would you like included in the ceremony? What would be meaningful for you?'

'It's up to Serena,' I wonder if this will be the deferring to her pattern of their life together but Ged is practical about replacing shopfront windows quickly.

Meanwhile, on legal advice from supermarket HQ, Ged removes the beer.

'Frankly it wasn't selling all that well. But I don't want the hoons to think they've won.'

In gratitude, Maddy is so thrilled by the success of her cause, she introduces her many supporters to shopping at Ged's store. Insurance covers the replacement window and stock. Locals are incensed by rioters using violence against their supermarket and Ged.

'I might add a few more organic brands,' offers Ged. 'In plain packaging. No religious symbols.'

'How about Easter hot cross buns?' teases Maddy. 'Or Christmas puddings…?'

Ged diversifies into organic foods, but only on one counter near the back wall. Then he adds a halal and a kosher section. Surprisingly business increases. Still smitten by the fifty-ish 'girl' who is so enthusiastic about her newly adopted culture and so keen on him. 'Isn't she charming?' says Ged to

every customer who asks about their forthcoming marriage...
'Never thought I'd marry, ...and a Buddhist.'

I'm more intrigued by Serena's instant conversions. And causes.

'Mc Meditation', Zac calls it. 'She can't answer my questions about whether Gran is a cat now, but the school kids like her so they pretend.'

'Do you have any religious requirements?' I ask Ged.

He shrugs. 'Not relevant to me.'

Serena's four earlier marriages appeared to correspond with the religion of her then current partner and lasted a few years on average, according to those dates. But she's not a bigamist.

'What might Buddhist style involve?' I ask. Religion isn't really a fashion style.

'Maybe some prayer flags?' Serena wasn't sure. 'My bridesmaid Maddy knows.' Since the successful boycott, Maddy had become the local Buddhist expert in the media. She explained to me about her term 'Nightstand Buddhism'.

'As in you might not say you're a Buddhist but you might be interested in meditation, or you might read books by the Dalai Lama. And keep spiritual books beside your bed or night stand.'

'Do certain colours matter?'

'Yes.' Maddy had done a bit of study during her Buddha Bottle campaign. 'The colours involved in Buddhism are Blue, Black, White, Red, Green, and Yellow, and each -- except Black -- are aligned to a specific Buddha. Green is the colour of balance and harmony. Linked to the head. Amoghasiddhi is the Buddha of the colour green. Green represents nature. Meditate on this colour to transform jealousy into the wisdom of accomplishment.'

I'm impressed. Maybe Maddy relies on Dr Google too? I'm not sure how Serena got Ged to propose after Maddy complained about the beer, but she accomplished that.

'I've got to find out about food for the Buddhist wedding.' My sister Bea likes a catering challenge. 'No beer.'

For a problem-solving sleuth-celebrant, Serena and Ged's ceremony was easy. Maddy organised some prayer flags and explained the meanings to me and to Serena. We wrote the ceremony together.

It didn't have much to do with Buddhist ideas, but it was about two gentle people who were going to live together with kindness. They exchanged the beautiful white scarves and blessings.

Serena looked so happy.

And Bea's SAGE's catering offered local apple juice in beautiful green tumblers which were not Buddha shaped.

The footy hoons did not form a guard of honour for the bride and groom, but they didn't interrupt the ceremony either. Students from Serena's meditation class held bunches of flowers as she came out of the hall. Zac delivered the flowers in the trike bike, and stayed for the cameras.

Art recorded the wedding for Channel Zero as an example of regional country town diversity supported by the census data showing Buddhism as a rapidly growing religion in Australia.

I suggested that. And as it was a slow news day, it went national.

Art introduced the film clip of the bride and groom flanked by prayer flags and children.' The Buddhist flag, first hoisted in 1885 in Sri Lanka, is a symbol of faith and peace used throughout the world to represent the Buddhist faith. The six colours of the flag represent the colours of the aura that emanated from the body of the Buddha when He attained Enlightenment under the Bodhi Tree.'

Watching Art's newscast, Zac says 'I wonder if people come back as people? Infinity Blooms is like…a sort of Buddhist name for a florist.'

Violet smiles, 'I just made it up. But thrilled my trike bike with the flowers was included in the background of the news.'

'Even if I was sitting on it?' says Zac.

Later I gave Ged his formal certificate of marriage, but I don't think he read the fine print or noticed how much information had to be squeezed into Serena's side.

'Another dead goldfish in the tank, Violet. Want me to look after it?' offers Zed. "Not sure where it's going.'

The Funeral of Fake ID

QUINN'S THEORY OF FUNERAL SECRETS

At a funeral, we acknowledge the life of the person and maybe the many identities, actions and secret lives of which the family and friends were unaware. For some a shock, for others a relief.

Collapsing on the seats outside Café SAGE, Art and I listen to the early morning conversations of the weekend cyclists around us. After jogging three kilometres, mainly uphill, I've run out of puff and need an excuse not to move for the next decade. Coffee! The café is so crowded; it will take a few minutes to be served. Excellent. But water first.

'Did you jog past the petanque pitch?' asks a twenty-something female cyclist looking at Art as he drinks from his water bottle. With a jolt, I recognise her.

'The piste?'

'Yeah, that's the proper name. The gravel part where the oldies play bowls.'

'No. We'll jog home that way. It's downhill. I thought the game was called bocce,' Art refills his water bottle from the café tap.

'Yes, if you're Italian. If you're French they call it petanque.'

'Have you got French relatives?' Art likes to find out about ancestry and especially from a pretty girl cyclist who asks questions. He's acting normally. But this is the girl he wanted me to meet for our possible new arrangement. I'm not feeling jealousy, just curiosity as to whether this is a coincidental meeting.

'No. But I'm studying languages at uni, French, Italian and Japanese. And doing Peace Studies in Politics.'

Must be in her first year. She is new enough to think others will be impressed.

'Saw Friday Barefoot Bowls at Dusk advertised. Thought they might be playing nude,' comments her male cyclist companion with a smile. 'Worth a look.'

The cyclist doesn't seem to be her boyfriend.

'Didn't happen,' Art adds with a smile, 'not this weekend anyway.'

'But something happened,' says the cyclist. 'I saw a police car at the ground. D'you know anything about that? '

Art shakes his head. We didn't then. Not until a few minutes later, when Claud rang me.

ﻪ

Cyclists prop their bikes against the fence. They unfold like tight Lycra- skin grasshoppers and look so much taller at full stretch height. The multi-lingual girl who spoke about the petanque is VERY tall. She smiles down at Art. And then at me.

'Great morning for a run or cycle. I'm Dee. You must be Quinn.'

I'm so used to looking at Art, that I forget he's short and think his height is the norm. So anyone else looks tall alongside him.

'Life is short and so am I,' Art responds when meeting newcomers and his height or lack of it isn't an issue for him. I'm used to hugging him at a certain angle and others feel strangely solid or too high. Despite his light frame, Art is in proportion and so it's only when he's standing alongside the tall, sweaty morning cyclists who are collecting their coffees,

I'm conscious of the height difference. My familiar becomes the norm.

Casual photos taken on mobiles remind me of our height difference, but in my favourite, cropped photos, I'm seated and Art stands behind me. Vanity I guess. Mine not his.

I just wish that I'd met Dee earlier, when Art first suggested I did.

ॐ

Café Sage's just-out-of-the-oven bread and aroma of coffee entice weekend joggers and cyclists who make it an after-run destination. Or in our case, a mid-jog excuse. Early customers are having breakfast coffee and freshly baked rolls with today's special eggs topped with Béarnaise sauce. Not many spaces left at the tables outside. Looking around, I smell the sweat. Mine and others. I think sweaty- but -self-conscious athletes prefer not to fog up the inside of the café, so they sit outside. The slight breeze cools my sweating legs and arms but I'm still thinking of ways to convince Art not to run any further at least in the next hour. Or a valid reason why I can opt out. I check my phone. No urgent messages. Pity.

Outside, Bea is chalking up her menu board. 'Date scones today Quinn. And green vegetable smoothies. Healthy stuff for you.'

The cyclists are refilling their water bottles too. Bea's café tap is the regular watering stop for those exercising. Even has a WELCOME sign above it. For dogs as well as people. The SAGE DOG water- bowls are lime-green too. Making it a dog-friendly café, is part of Bea's new branding.

'Notice you're wearing your SAGE apron Bea. What happened to the signature rolls with sage?' I've got my breath back now. And I prefer eating to jogging.

'Recycled to the chooks.' Bea shrugs.

Lucky chooks. Those rolls were a rare failure in Bea's baking experiments.

'Last week's creamy Vanilla slices were to die for in the best possible way Bea,' says Art who is NOT breathless and he's run the same distance as me. But he is sweating. Beads of moisture on his forehead which he brushes away with the back of his hand. 'I've just about worked those million calories off.'

Inside, the TV news –reader comments about secret Eastern European files released about wartime collaborators. A world 50 years away. But I notice Dee the Peace Studies cyclist is watching the news as she collects their drinks.

My mobile rings. Claud from the Village. 'This is a work-call Quinn. Sad news. Remember Rocky Kovac with all the rocks in front of his unit? Flora used to be his next door neighbour.'

'Of course.' How could I forget Rocky? The eccentric rock collector.

'He passed away last night and according to his wishes, The Village is to arrange his funeral. I spoke to the funeral arranger. Would you be willing to be the celebrant? It would be in our chapel venue.'

'Does he have any family?'

'That's what I'm trying to work out now. Only a distant Kovac cousin listed. Rocky was single. There will be an issue with the coroner too.'

'Why?'

'Rocky's body was found at the petanque piste last night. A late evening jogger called the police. And now the coroner's people have taken the body and cordoned the area.'

'Did he have a heart attack?' I ask. That's the most common sudden death for Village residents.

'No, someone hit him with a boule. Fatal. On the temple.'

'An accidental throw?'

'Unlikely. That's why the police car was there,' says Claud. 'Now it's a taped- off crime scene.'

My phone is on loud and Art can hear Claud's voice. He raises his eyebrows and whispers, 'What time was he found?'

'9-30 ish last night.'

'Got dark about 8 o'clock,' Art whispers. 'Barefoot Bowlers would have gone home then.'

'Was he practising alone?' I ask Claud.

'Easier for us if he had been. Then it would be an accident. But he couldn't throw a boule at himself with that kind of force. Someone else must have been involved.'

According to French custom, petanque is played with a glass of red wine in your other hand. But oldies have enough trouble balancing themselves for a throw as the metallic bowls are quite heavy. I can't imagine anyone flexible enough to kill Rocky with a well placed boule.

'Were any of the bowlers still around?' I ask. 'I thought their matches finished at dusk, when it was too dark to see the jack.'

Barefoot Bowling was an attempt to update the old fashioned image of bowls. Cheaper too. They don't have to buy a white uniform. Or shoes. Can play anywhere on gravel or grass. But they are not naked.

'They've got floodlights now. The Village paid for them as so many residents are keen on the game. Gentle exercise.'

Murder is not gentle exercise. Around us, cyclists are still chatting. And in the background the TV noise goes on about global atrocities. Strange how someone can die and ordinary stuff like drinking green vegetable smoothies continues.

'Ok, let's jog back home via the petanque piste, 'I suggest to Art. 'Claud said he's going to meet us there. I'll need to sort out the paperwork.'

We cancel our coffee and my green smoothie. Together we jog downhill. The yellow police tape cordons the area. A policeman is on guard. Claude is waiting for us.

Immediately I can tell from his face. Claud is very upset about another suspicious death in the Village. He feels guilty as if it's his fault that such deaths should happen on his patch.

'Only a few months ago we lost Flora,' Claud had been genuinely fond of his ex-Boss.

'The wonderful Tawny Femme Formidable.' I say. 'I miss her too.'

Flora was impaled under the roller door in the garage shared with Rocky. The verdict was death by misadventure but locals had continuing suspicions. Especially about her family being involved in her death.

'Those units will be getting a reputation for being unlucky. Two suspicious deaths. Quite Agatha Christie-ish,' Claud regrets.

'Might Rocky's death have been an accident?' suggests Art.

'Or was he a target for any particular reason at this time?' I ask.

Claud shrugs, 'Rocky was known to cheat. Despite using a walking frame. He'd kick his boule a bit closer, or pick it up quickly before others had a chance to check. Most move slower than him. At first they used to let him judge the distances because he walked faster with his frame. But then they noticed he always won, and got suspicious.'

'Cheating is not sufficient reason to kill someone,' Art says. I agree. Especially when no petanque championships are scheduled in the next week.

'Where did he come from originally? Wasn't it that country mentioned on the TV news yesterday? The one which released the secret war –crimes documents online?' I suggest. 'Some embargo was lifted.'

Claud nods. 'Yes. Have you ever looked closely at the labels and stories on his rocks? Even got his version of his autobiography chiselled there on a plaque with dates and places. Probably a work of fiction.'

'Could Rocky have a murky political past?' I ask. 'Could he have upset someone then?'

'Maybe in the war, decades ago. Who would know about that around here? Why act on it now?'

'Someone threw that boule hard at his head. And they knew where to hit. The temple is the most vulnerable part. Look at the blood on the gravel. There's the boule target.' Art points to the bright yellow jack. 'They weren't aiming at that. They got Rocky.'

The cochonnet which most called the 'jack' was at the other end of the gravel. Rocky's heavy bowls bag was still sitting open within the yellow-cordoned area. A police officer was on guard nearby.

'Heavy bowls bag for an elderly man to carry?' I query.

'He had a shelf and hook on his walking frame.' Claud explains, 'Rocky wasn't the most popular person in the Village. Used to bore everyone about his rocks. But that's no reason to kill him.'

'Then what would be the motive?' Art asks.

'Things get out of proportion once your world shrinks, with age and declining mobility,' Claud sounds hesitant as if he doesn't believe his own words. 'Competitive residents even measure who is closest to the jack with a measuring tape. But they're too frail to throw hard enough to kill Rocky. And WHY would they?'

'To kill someone with a heavy, metallic boule, the size of a bomb…just to win a game!' Art exclaims.' Not likely.'

Claud regards me as a fellow problem-solver. So he shares confidentially,' Now there's another problem. Sorting out his bloody rocks. Apparently a few are quite valuable. So I can't just get the earthmoving bloke in to dig them out. Trouble is I don't know which ones…so we'll need to have the minerals valued.'

'Who do you think was involved in Rocky's death?'

Claud shrugs. "I don't know. But I do know it is now MY problem.'

ॐ

'Excuse me. I'm looking for the person in charge.' Seventy-ish, he has a faint accent. Grey beard, well trimmed. Grey cap. Well cut trousers with polished shoes. Expensive but well worn jacket and with an air of quiet authority.

Claud stands up, and puts out his hand.

'I'm Claud. I look after the residencies at Everest.'

'I'm Kovac, the cousin of the deceased, Tomo Kovac. I was asked to identify him. By the police.'

'Oh. Our condolences.' Claud slips into his official Village role as manager.

'With the police, I've been to the morgue. But this man is not my cousin. He has fake I.D. He has my cousin's name and his papers, but not his face.'

'What?' Claud is shocked. 'It's the wrong man?'

Kovac's face is stern. 'But I recognize him. He did come

from our village. He was a collaborator during the war. We all hated him. I think he took my cousin's papers and emigrated pretending to be him. So I have identified him but with his real name. Josef Smit.'

ॐ

Some of my best insights come in the shower.

As I towel myself dry, a thought niggles at me.

Did the killer want to remove Josef Smit a.k.a. Rocky or the original real Tomo Kovac? Had one or both committed some kind of war crime? Was it a revenge killing?

Art has been online. 'I've done a bit of checking on the Kovac name. If he came out of a warzone, he might have had fake I.D. Often if the town hall which held the records was demolished or over-run, those who had political connections and needed to emigrate would assume the identity of a local who died in the war. Hard to prove otherwise. Then once they entered Australia on those documents, they needed to maintain the fiction.'

'Can you check if there's a death certificate for Tomo Kovac?' I ask. 'With dates that fit.'

'Why don't we ask Cousin Kovac? You'll have to speak to him about arranging the funeral anyway,' suggests Art.

'If the deceased is not his cousin, he won't be at the funeral.'

'Hadn't thought about that. You're right. Claud will have to do it.'

ॐ

I'm a little uncomfortable about asking him questions. I'm the celebrant, and it seems that now he is NOT my client.

'Did you have any contact with Kovac?'

Cousin Kovac takes off his grey cap and reveals a full head of well cut hair. Caps often mask baldness in the seventy plus age group. This man presents as 'in control'. But I think he is masking something tragic from the past.

'No contact. Not with my cousin. For years I have been working abroad in remote regions. I'm an engineer. And I thought none of my family were left after our village was razed.'

'So who was Josef Smit, the one with false I.D. based on your cousin Tomo's documents?'

'Smit was a collaborator from our village. This week, the embargo was lifted on the crimes documents. It's fifty years since it happened. That's when I started tracking survivors. And found the Everest address.'

I remember the TV news in SAGE cafe!

'Collaborators were listed. Josef Smit was listed as dead. But my cousin Tomo Kovac who was NOT a collaborator, was listed as alive and I suspected he was dead. So I came looking for your Rocky. I thought he might have used Tomo's papers to vanish. And he did.'

'Could there have been a mistake. Often officials transcribed one letter wrong and then this is repeated on all official documents,' says Art.

I add, 'This happens with some baby's names when the father has too many drinks before he registers his new offspring...'

Cousin Kovac explains. 'Australians find it difficult to spell or pronounce our names. So they shorten them. And there are lots of different versions of our surname. But I found Smit using our family name. That made me suspicious.'

'What happened with Rocky…er… I'm not sure what to call him now.'

'Kovac is Slovak for blacksmith but we were Serbian. Family names are no joking matter.'

'Any country with neighbours on all borders gets over-run a lot. They become the battleground. With inter-marriage they absorb the food and customs of the powerful conqueror. Names change. Often they forget who introduced what. Like Macedonians claim the bagpipes.' Art grins.

'Is that funny?' asks Cousin Kovac.

'I apologise,' says Art. 'Maybe not appropriate at the moment.'

'But why did his death occur now?' I ask Cousin Kovac.

'When I first visited Everest, he was not home. But I saw his labels on the rocks in front of his unit. He had made a story about his courage. All lies. He was no hero. I was furious that he stole the name of my cousin. And his reputation as a genuine hero of the Underground.

'Watching the TV news I realised. Josef Smit had taken my cousin's life. And what was worse, he had stolen his future life too. My cousin Tomo was a brave man who worked in the political Underground. He was betrayed by Josef Smit who was a collaborator.

'How can you have sympathy for a man who steals the identity of the man he….betrayed.'

'If you don't mind me asking, how did your cousin die?'

'Smit killed him at the end of the war… he had an uncontrollable temper then and now.

'Yesterday I challenged Smit. He knew who I was. As boys we looked like brothers. Now I look as my cousin Tomo would have looked, if he had lived. Smit thought I was a ghost from his past. I was.'

'Where did you challenge Smit?'

'As he was going to kill me at the piste.'

❧

'Why do you think Cousin Kovac killed Rocky with the boule?' asks Art. We were back home now, trying to make sense of events. 'He doesn't seem remorseful.'

'It was the timing which was important. Remember that news item it would have been on the late news on Friday night. The Kovac village would have been mentioned.' I say.

'What do you think really happened?' asks Art as he pours us a drink each.

'Do you want to hear my sympathetic-to-Cousin version? It hangs on Cousin hoping that his real cousin was still alive, but discovering that not only had Smit assumed the fake ID, he had also killed the original Tomo fifty years ago.'

Art nods. 'I'm glad my geni research helped you.'

'Cousin Kovac tracked down Rocky at Everest Village and hoped to see his real cousin, thinking there had been a genuine mix up of identity by the authorities and a slim chance that Tomo was alive and living as Rocky Kovac. Right?'

'Yes, that's pretty much what I worked out.'

'Then he was shocked to discover via the TV news of secret war crimes lists released that it was Smit who killed Tomo years ago in their village.

At the same time, Rocky realized that Cousin Kovac was the only relative left who could identify him as a fake and a murderer.'

Art is ahead of me. I hadn't thought of Rocky's reason for attacking the Cousin at the petanque pitch. I had thought it was the other way around.

'You can understand why Cousin was upset.'

'Cousin Kovac wanted revenge. The secret documents about collaborators released this week, revealed his real cousin had been murdered by Rocky, who switched identity. Rocky assumed the fake ID of Kovac and managed to get into Australia as a displaced person.

Cousin comes looking to check on real Kovic and finds the FAKE who attacks him. Provoked, Cousin defends himself at the petanque piste with the nearest weapon which is the boule.'

Art's mobile rings. 'Here, talk to her. Quinn is beside me now. ' Art hands me his mobile. 'Dee tell Quinn what you told me.'

I hadn't known Art was on such friendly terms with Dee. But maybe he was just looking for more subjects to interview on Channel Zero.

Dee says, 'That's the man we saw heading towards the petanque, when we rode past on Friday night. I remember his grey cap because I thought it was so old fashioned, like my Grandad.'

'Thankyou Dee,' I switch off the phone and then realise I should have handed it back to Art first.

Now there's a witness who can place Cousin Kovac at the petanque. But she is unnecessary.

'I hit him with the boule, in self defence. I told the police that,' admits Cousin Kovac. 'They have charged me.'

We are left, standing outside the rock garden.

'I guess a garage sale of his rocks are out of the question?' Art attempts to lighten Claud's sombre mood. 'Or an auction? You can't really have a Garage Sale and expect buyers to carry away their own pet rock. Maybe rock music in the background?'

Claud gives a wry smile.

'Need help with the eulogy?' Art offers. 'My 'geni' research skills are available, free to you.'

I shake my head. 'Thanks but no thanks. Maybe I can just use visuals of the rock garden as a memorial. There are some beautiful minerals there amongst the fake I.D.'

Such a challenge to write the eulogy for Rocky a.k.a. Josef Smit. Difficulty of acknowledging the life of a killer in an appropriate way. It's really the funeral of a Fake ID.

Quinn's Theory of Funeral Secrets

At a funeral, we acknowledge the life of the person and maybe the many identities, actions and secret lives of which the family and friends were unaware. For some a shock, for others a relief.

Night Cap

THEORY OF SPECIAL RELATIVITY IS EINSTEIN'S famous equation $E = mc^2$. In this formula E is energy, m is mass, and c is the constant speed of light.

My version is a bit different. $E = mc^2$. Emotion = marriage multiplied by commitment doubled.

Nightcap has more than one meaning. There's the drink, the hat and the deadly version. As we discovered recently.

Dan is my fairly new brother-in-law whom I married late last year. I was the celebrant. Bea was the bride. Dan was the groom, looking very smart in his uniform. Then he had to leave, soon after the wedding on some military tour to Afghanistan. We're never too sure what secret military electronic stuff Dan does. And we're not supposed to ask. So we don't.

His absences are a bit hard on Bea as she's only in occasional Skype contact with her new husband. In between, Bea is expanding Café Sage with new menus, lime- green décor plus niche catering for local clients (including mine) with gluten-free, dairy-intolerant or even fructose-free fabulous platters. Café Sage has gone from a dis-used corner shop to THE local meet & eat place. A bit of serious competition now for others in the area. 'Pet-free' is her new policy but that's ambiguous as I keep mentioning to my little sister.

'Bea, does it mean no pets, and that your café is free of pets?'

'No, Quinn.'

'Free for pets? Don't the owners have to pay if accompanied by an animal?'

'No. It means they are welcome.'

'Inside?'

'No, outside. Where I put the pet water bowls. The Pet Free Zone.'

Bea laughs at me. ' Don't fuss Quinn. I'm sure the pets can understand. 'In' or 'out' is pretty simple even for dropouts from Dog Obedience School. Or control-freak celebrants.'

I decide not to hear that, because mostly I'm fond of my younger sister. Aware my fussing with words annoys some people. And I do know what 'pedantic' means.

In situations with official forms where there's only Male or Female gender options, I suggest extra boxes for Other. Or Diverse. I always complain with language reasons. Not just gender.

'Pets are not only dogs or cats. There are diverse pets. You might get the odd snake, rat or Bengal tiger-cat,' I suggest. 'In Parisian cafes you can carry your cat or dog in your shoulder bag.'

Bea nods. 'True. But this isn't Paris. And not many pet snakes around here. A few poisonous locals in the bush.'

Frankly I'm not fussed whether pets can read or not. As long as dogs don't lift their legs at awkward moments during my ceremonies. It did happen last month, in the background of a wedding photo when the dog pissed on the bride's lacy, long train and no-one realised until later. Ruined the shot (and the dress) but then some guest put it up online with a caption 'Dog–day' and had lots of hits.

'Saw the Dog- day photo online,' says Bea. 'But I won't pin it in the café.'

Café SAGE has a community noticeboard behind the till.

Mainly cartoons. Or For Sale or Swap offers. And a flourishing website attracting online orders.

'Thanks.'

Not my best advertisement. But I couldn't control that. Nor the weather that day. It poured. Not sure if the photographer -guest with a million friends on Facebook knew 'dog day' meant a sultry, hot afternoon when Sirius, the Dog Star, rises at the same time as the sun. A period marked by lethargy, inactivity, or indolence. Probably not.

Back to real life. Or at least the fictional world of gender-free, super-hero game- playing. Although Bea has a Gluten-Free bar in the café, I'll not be using a Gender-Free Zone sign for the Tournament area. Unnecessary.

Locally, this was going to be a big, long weekend. The Motives game- players have their annual LONG PLAY Tournament across three days. Really good business for Café Sage to get this event as other regions wanted to host it. I've been hoping that no unexpected funerals would make me cancel. Bea had promised to partner me. Embarrassing to admit that your sister is the best player around, but terrific if she is on your team. But then things change quickly.

'Sorry Quinn, I'm going to have to drop out of the Motives Tournament,' says Bea, checking her phone. 'Dan is coming back at the weekend. Unexpectedly. Only for the three days. And I'm going to meet him in Melbourne for a romantic long weekend. Can't turn down that offer. Never know when he'll be back again. But it's really bad timing for my business. I need to be here so the Tournament goes well enough for them to return next year.'

'That's okay. Go as soon as you can. I'll look after things.'

I didn't expect to deal with mass poisoning.

Quite a few families in this town have F.I.F.O (Fly in

fly out) partners who work for extended periods in remote regions. Always takes them a few days to resettle into ordinary domestic life on their days back home. Too used to telling others what to do. Not keen on putting out the bins or fixing stuff around the house. Power balances change. Others in the household have managed without them. They feel superfluous at home. Then they fly back to work where their status matters.

Dan and Bea are a new couple and haven't had to negotiate babies or teenagers complicating re-unions. So absences and returns are more romantic for them: a series of honeymoons. Maybe if they have kids it will be different. But I'm not putting that pressure on any couple as Art's parents do with us. Unsure if having kids is viable for me. I'm not keen. And now there's the issue of Dee as Art's sexual partner. Kids are not an issue there. That's just a physical relationship. We're now in a polyamorous relationship. An amicable one, where I allow them time together.

'I do understand you have to go, Bea.' Dan's world is dangerously real and our game is playing fiction with super heroes of indeterminate gender in worlds beyond ours. Even if at heart I'm a pacifist, I like planning the campaign strategies. So I offer. 'Would you like me to run the Tournament?'

'Yes. But I don't expect you to do the catering or run the Café.'

We both agree that Bea is the cook in our family. I am the eater. And it's going to stay that way. She rings around to get a locum chef to cover the weekend. Everybody is booked up.

'Short notice. All the good ones are gone. Guy is my last resort. I went to catering school with him. He's a bit slapdash.'

Since Guy's recently returned from backpacking in off-the-beaten-track Asia, he's broke and needs the money. Coming immediately.

'Does he need a bed at our place? Where will he be staying?' I ask.

'In my flat.'

Normally Bea lives behind SAGE Café. Most of her energies go into the café, so the flat is fairly basic with recycled furniture. House-sitting, I slept on her saggy bed once, and never again. And her kitchen chairs wobble. Her best chairs are in the café.

'Guy travels light. He can sleep anywhere. Average cook but works long shifts in hospitality 'til he makes enough money to move on. His hobby is foraging local plants for salads and hotpots. He'll be here soon. We'll have an hour for the hand-over and then I'll go.'

Bea gives me a spare set of the Café keys. 'Everything is prepared. Guy won't be able to mess up much. He's got a bit of a reputation for stuff-ups.'

'Glad you've got someone to fill in.'

Guy is a ginger haired, wiry man with weather-beaten eyes. Could be any age. 'Bea's flat is great,' he enthuses when I ask if he's settled in. Obviously he hasn't slept the night on that bed yet. He travels with a well-used backpack but has brought his own chef knives, which he unrolls from their leather tooled carry bag.

'Have any trouble getting those through airport security?' I ask. They are VERY sharp.

'Declared as tools of trade.'

'Oh.'

He accepts the lime-green SAGE Café apron Bea left.

'Would help-yourself soup be a good idea for the players?'

he suggests. 'Mushroom? French onion? Vietnamese Pho with noodles, green onion and bean sprouts?'

'Sure.'

Guy suggests extras from his recent travels. 'Thai basil, lime wedges, hoisin sauce, and chilli-garlic sauce on the side?'

'Great.'

Guy was in the same cooking school as Bea, but he is not in the same class with her attention to detail. As I found out, too late. He seems to be very keen on adding fresh, local ingredients and went out foraging for herbs and mushrooms. While jogging at dusk, Art sees him with a flat basket and digging stick wandering happily in the bushlands behind Everest Residential Community indiscriminately collecting local plants for his salads.

'Is it ok to eat some of those weeds and fungi Guy is gathering? I'm always a bit careful,' Art says.

Frankly I don't know much about local mushrooms, but Bea does. I suggest Guy call Bea to check. She was so keen to see Dan, that maybe Guy as last minute locum was a compromise. Usually the café came first.

Meanwhile I set up the back of the café as Tournament HQ, with a side table of slow cooking pots for the self-serve hot snacks and drinks in anticipation of those all- nighters expected. Numbers are up.

'Guy, did you ring Bea to check on the mushrooms?' I ask, looking at the foraging basket. Fungi. Mushrooms. Lots of green weeds I don't know. And a few blackberries. They look safe.

'Been a bit busy,' says Guy chopping ingredients enthusiastically. Light reflects from his speedy knives. He's messy, there's stuff all over the bench.

So I text Bea. Less intrusive. Offer to send an ID photo of the food.

She calls back immediately.

'The edible straw mushrooms used in Asian cooking are quite safe to eat. The problem is they look a bit like Death Cap mushrooms. Death caps have amatoxin which attacks your enzymes which produce your DNA. The poison can trigger liver failure. And you can die.' Bea warns. 'Got to go now, Dan is here. Check with Dr G2 the pharmacist if you are worried.'

Understandably, Bea is a bit occupied with her new husband. I should have sent the mushroom ID photo then. My fault.

Guy shrugs. 'These look okay to me. I've used similar ones before.'

That's how my in-laws were inadvertently poisoned with night cap mushrooms in the soup.

ه♥

Art had invited his parents to stay and unfortunately they chose this long weekend. That was a BIG mistake. Not just because of the Tournament and Bea away. But we needed to sort out a few family issues. It's difficult when you are a genderqueer couple unlikely to produce grandkids for an elderly couple who desire them. Bea and Dan are possible parents, but since our father died last year, there's no pressure from my side of the family. Only from Art's side. I'm not planning on becoming a parent, nor acquiring a nephew or niece. But I know Art's parents want grandkids with Art as the Dad. Unlikely. Unless he has a surrogate.

ه♥

I call into 'Infinity Blooms' for some floral insurance.

'Could I buy one of your Apology Pot Plants, please Violet?'

Violet is preparing several bunches of long stemmed roses. Ruby red, with fresh green leaves and the perfume wafts towards me. 'Infinity Blooms' has a pile of bouquet orders waiting on the counter to be delivered by trike bike basket. Each skilfully gift- wrapped in tones of the flowers inside. Shades of red. Others range from lemon to amber and gold. Cycling is Violet's daily exercise even if Zac is always offering to replace her as delivery person. But she doesn't trust her delicate blooms to Zac's driving or cycling. A bit like my sister who is worried about leaving a locum.

'Stunning roses. Have you met Guy, the temporary chef?'

'Too busy here.' The yet-to-be delivered pile of bouquets is growing rapidly.

I love watching Violet's skilful hands twisting stems and arranging petals. She threads ribbon and ties so elegantly.

'Lots of urgent flower orders?'

'Dr G ordered seven bunches of roses for his wife. It's a significant anniversary for them. He wanted them delivered to her pharmacy up the street as a surprise. But now he's coming to get them himself, any minute.' Bea finishes the sixth bunch, zipping the ribbon ends into a sophisticated curl with her scissors. Then she slips her love poem in with the flowers. 'Only do that for the special customers.'

'Do you want me to write his full name on the invoice for you? I can copy it from his business card.'

I always think it's rude not to use a person's full name because it's culturally difficult to say, or spell, but their Indian surname is a challenge for locals and Violet especially. He's known as Dr G the doctor, and she's Dr G2 the pharmacist.

And a favourite with locals. Endlessly patient. Even over mixups with prescriptions.

Just then Dr G dashes in, still wearing his stethoscope, name tag and white coat. 'I'll take all the roses with me now for my wife.'

'Romantic,' says Violet. 'Do you want your receipt now or later?'

'Want me to write it for you?' I offer to Violet. 'Are there two 'a's in that? 'I ask the doctor who gives a little smile, and indicates his name-tag.

'Gangopadhyaya, our surname is West Bengali, but we're ok with Dr G and Dr G2. Unless it's legal stuff. I'll just use my credit card to pay for the flowers.'

I don't know Dr G2's first name and she's been here so long that I can't ask her. I will get their surname right in future. Gang-o-pad-hy-aya.

'We've been married seven years,' he says, keying in his card.

The same time Art and I have been together.

'Her name is Gulab which means rose. That's why I always buy her roses. Seven years. Seven bunches.'

'Hope you can carry enough flowers for later anniversaries,' Violet arranges the bunches in his arms. 'Congratulations. And hope you make it to your 40th, 50th and 100th. And that she likes the poem card.'

'Thank you Violet.' I notice Dr G didn't say 'soul-mate' once.

Quinn's Theory of Soul-Mates
The number of times the word soul-mates is used in public is in reverse proportion to the number of months the relationship lasts.

Dr G dashes out and Violet turns to me.

'Now, who have you insulted that you need my Apology Pot plant?'

'Nobody yet. But Art's parents are visiting this weekend. And I'm sure to upset them. Even if I just write a friendly card on the flowers, for Perce and Rose from your daughter-in-law, it will upset them.'

'From your daughter-out-law?' Violet suggests. 'From your son's partner?'

It's easier when you have a recognised role like celebrant. Much harder when you are the partner of their son.

'How does Art introduce you to his relatives?'

'He doesn't. They just nod usually or talk about the weather.'

'Why don't you write From Quinn and let them work out your relationship. Isn't that why they are coming?' Violet sorts out her multi-coloured pot plants and chooses a red one. 'Maybe I could offer you a discount on multiple Apology Pot Plants. Sounds like you might need them.'

'I'll take half a dozen.'

'Well, if you don't insult anyone, you can always plant them in your front garden,' suggests Violet.

Art's parents have recently become Grey Nomads and prefer to have a destination to aim for. We are the destination, or Art is. And there's just about enough room in our front garden to park a caravan if we tackle the weeds before they arrive. And fix the fence, which I have done. Even painted it.

'A red pot plant from Violet. One of her Apology Plants? Oh, did you get it for my mother?' asks Art looking at me.

I'm trying. 'Your mother doesn't know they are called Violet's Apology Pot Plants unless you tell her. It's a beautiful red plant for the caravan. I'm just getting in first. I'm sure to say something over the weekend which upsets your mother or your father.'

'Highly likely,' says Art. 'If I don't say something to upset them first.'

'I bought multiple plants,' I admit. 'Red, purple, gold, white, blue-ish and a sort of pink one.'

Art laughs. 'Insurance?'

ॐ

The mushroom soup looks appetising in the slow cooker pots. People help themselves in-between games. Bread rolls. Cheeses. Cold meats. Dips. Interesting pickled vegetables. Unusual salads in shades of green with occasional red peppers, purple cabbage or orange carrot. Even beetroot, my favourite… Initially, it looks like Chef Guy has catered well for the Tournament. Bea needn't have worried. Even if the kitchen looks like a vegetable peelings bomb went off. Very messy. But customers won't see that.

The problems came six hours later.

ॐ

I enjoy timetabling the contestants. 'Motives' is growing fast. Almost a business instead of a hobby. Even notice a familiar name on the entries. Xavier has re-entered the world of fantasy and diverse super-heroes. After detouring into the Kingdom of Nappies and Baby Feeds.

'Grandmother Anastasia offered to babysit little Askie for a day. She's so delighted the baby has her name.' Xavier grins. 'For me, a bit too much family reality lately. I need a dose of fantasy and power and other worlds. But I can only manage the Saturday. Not the whole weekend.'

Unfortunately Xavier spent some of his weekend in Emergency. Inadvertently, he did some research for his next game.

ॐ

Players are enjoying 'Motives' at the back of the café. Fairly quiet as they are concentrating, but with occasional bursts of conversation as they share the strategies they used in each set. We don't have a meal break, they just help themselves from the food table, so I'm not sure how much each ate. Or from which pot.

Later that was important. When the Emergency doctor asked me how many helpings, I didn't know.

Out front, Guy was serving weekend café customers. Even my in-laws Perce and Rose dropped in for an ice cream. As a hobby, Perce taste-tests ice creams at each location they stay. I think Rose may be ice creamed-out. She has a coffee.

'Which brand of ice cream do you prefer?' Perce asks Guy who is multi-tasking at the counter, juggling coffee, hot savouries, sandwiches, smoothies and ice creams. Plus operating the till. During the rush periods, I help him.

'Quite like Purity ice cream,' says Guy nodding towards the freezer stacked with iced treats.

'Really,' says Perce. 'Why?'

'Better quality,' says Guy. 'Local. 'Nibbles', my last place where I worked before I went overseas, used to stock them.'

'You might be right there.' Perce is looking more cheerful now. He peers more closely at the range displayed in the freezer. Nods approvingly at familiar packaging.

'Wasn't that place 'Nibbles' in trouble for a Salmonella outbreak?' asks Perce. 'Bad eggs used in the cooking?'

'Yes, just before I went overseas. Didn't think most people knew about that.'

'I like to keep up to date in my industry,' says Perce.'Even if I have retired, I still own the Purity business. Where did you see the Purity ice cream in Asia?'

'I found it in Malaysia first...' Guy whizzes up green vegetable smoothies for the couple sitting near the window.

'Really didn't know we exported it there... Pirated brands can be a problem sometimes.'

'We?'

'Used to be a dairy famer. Then we moved into gourmet ice creams. Yoghurt Smoothies and so on.'

'I thought you were a Grey Nomad?'

'I am. We are.'

'So why did you stop here?'

'My son lives here, with his...er...partner.'

'You mean Quinn? Bea the café owner is Quinn's sister.'

'Er yes.'

This was the moment when Guy might ruin my future with my in-laws and I'd have to start buying Violet's Apology Pot Plants in bulk.

So I turn around from sorting notes in the till and interrupt.

'Maybe you'd like to try the mushroom soup Perce? Guy added local cream to that. Then I'll show you how Motives works. Come down the back with me. So many teams playing there.'

ॐ

Xavier was the first to be raced to hospital with stomach pains, vomiting and diarrhoea. Then Perce, my father-in-law. And his wife Rose. Closely followed by six other Motives players. And even the chef Guy. He was really bad. The ambulance took him.

'Close the Tournament and the café,' Art rings me from Emergency at the hospital. 'I think Guy mistook Nights Caps for the edible straw mushrooms used in Asian cooking. He'd be familiar with them. But he's so ill, I can't ask him.'

Now I know what that phrase, 'my heart sinks' means. And I promised Bea I'd look after things. Not poison her customers. And ruin her business reputation.

'I'll ask Dr G2 about the mushrooms. A chemist would know. And I'll check on all the people here, then send them home.'

I switch the OPEN/CLOSE sign and shut the café just as Dr G2 arrives in a hurry. Players have already left. She knocks on the door. I open up.

'Quinn. I got a Health Department message that there might be a problem with poisoning. I wanted to check the soup you have left here. And the preparation area.'

'Please do.' I show her. 'Appreciate any help.'

'Who had big helpings? Or more than one helping?' Dr G2 looks very worried.

'Xavier. And maybe Guy because he was tasting in the kitchen.'

'If you've eaten a large meal of Deathcaps, the symptoms could start as early as 6 hours after the meal. But usually 10-16 hours. Soup would dilute the mushrooms. And depends how much you ate.' Dr G2's brown eyes are concerned.

'What are the symptoms?' I ask. This is getting worse by the minute. I haven't called Bea yet. I know I should. I'm just putting off telling her the bad news. She can't do anything from where she is.

'The first symptoms are stomach pains, vomiting and diarrhoea.'

'Xavier has those. How long does it last?'

'A day or two. The "recovery" period may last for 2 or 3 days. Then the terminal phase of 3-5 days.'

'Terminal? That means the end?' Suddenly I realize the implications not just for Xavier but all Bea's customers.

'Yes. Pains, vomiting and diarrhoea come back accompanied by jaundice. Coma and death occur between one and two weeks after eating the mushroom. Death is by liver failure, often with kidney failure too.' Dr G2's tone is neutral as if she's moved into professional mode.

I am in shock. 'Are they all going to die?'

'If you get medical help soon enough, they'll be all right. So the hospital is the best place.'

'I took people there immediately. With a time lag like that, we may have more people getting sick?'

'Yes, but the hospital will be checking already. And the Health Department. Their people will be here soon. '

'How do the poisons work?' We go inside and I close the door again.

'The nucleus of a human cell contains the DNA that is the instruction book for the cell and tells it how to work. The deadly compounds within the Deathcap stop the cell reading its own instruction book and the cell dies. If enough cells in a human liver or kidney are affected and die, then there will be liver or kidney failure - and then death.'

'Cheerful news.' Should I call Bea now, or wait until I get to the hospital? Should I call each of the players who has already gone home? There might be worse news by then.

I check online. Two people who ate poisonous deathcap

mushrooms at a New Year's Eve party died in a Sydney hospital. Eating just one mushroom can be fatal.

The café phone rings. 'Hello, Café Sage. Quinn speaking.'

'This is the hospital, Director of Emergency speaking.'

I try to concentrate on the details so I can share them with Bea.

The hospital has run tests. 'Night cap poisoning' is their conclusion.

'Dr G2, can you help me check on the mushrooms in this kitchen?' I indicate.

So helpful to have a chemist here. And she's the type of person you don't feel embarrassed to ask for help. Even with Guy's mess in the preparation area.

'Bea would normally keep this pristine,' I say as an apology for the chaos.

We check all the ingredients left in the chaotic kitchen. We find a half-full basket of mushrooms and other fungi in the cupboard. And then DrG2 examines the stockpots.

'Depends how many he used in the soup,' she says.' Varied strength in different pots. He must have made up more than one soup. And more than one batch.'

'Why do it?'

'It must have been an accident. Why else would Guy have eaten the soup himself? Unless one batch was not poisonous and that's the one he thought he ate.' I say. ' Surely Guy didn't mean to poison the customers or the Motives players?'

Could someone else be trying to wreck Café Sage's reputation? This thought had troubled me from the start. But who would have a motive? That word again! I do have regrets which I share with Dr G2.

'I wish Guy had checked with you earlier. Bea told him to do that.' I say. 'And I wish I'd sent the ID photo earlier.'

Dr G2 has a very reassuring manner, but she's also firm. 'Let's just deal with the practicalities. Quinn, you must ring Bea.'

'Yes.' I know. I have to call Bea. She's the owner of the café. She has a right to know. But she's also my little sister and I'd like to solve the problem for her first. But I can't. So the call can't be put off any longer. '

I dial her mobile. 'Bea?'

'What's wrong Quinn?'

I explain. There's a gasp.

'What?' Bea is incredulous.' I go away for three days and half the town is poisoned after eating at my café. With soup prepared by MY locum chef.'

'Not the whole town. All the ones who were affected are safely in the hospital Emergency ward. But with the delay in responses, there could be more.'

'I'll come straight home. Meet you at the hospital.'

'Ten people have been affected to different degrees, partly dependent upon how much they ate. Your father-in-law had a much smaller serve of the mushroom prepared soup,' says the doctor in charge of the hospital emergency ward. 'And your mother- in -law had very little.'

That was a relief. I was worried Art's dad would think the poisoning was deliberate and aimed at them because it's my sister's CAFÉ and her chef's catering. As if my side of the family were trying to get rid of him.

'They're just resting in the recovery ward.'

There are a few familiar faces. Motives players who look a bit washed out. Understandably. And my in-laws sitting up on beds either side of Art on the chair in between. Art gives me a rueful smile.

'Dad's had a bit of experience with industrial espionage. Iced sweet recipes copied. Pirated. Not quite like secret herbs &spices recipes, but…' Art explains. 'He wants to talk to you.'

Another problem?

Perce sits up in bed, jotting notes, a bit like I do. 'Blackmail or industrial espionage? ' He greets me.

'What?'

'Industrial espionage is always a possibility,' says Perce. 'Did Café Sage have any competitors? With this Motives Tournament business. Would anyone have wanted to attract that to their premises for the next Tournament? They seem to be a cluey 'cashed up 'group with considerable potential. Just a thought.'

With a shock I realize. In a strange sort of way, Perce is enjoying himself. He's centre of attention and has a problem to solve. He's not just a Grey Nomad in transit. He tests his theories on me.

'With all these Motives players on site, I wondered if anyone had deliberately poisoned us. Playing a game. Just to test reactions and how people would act in an emergency?'

I shake my head. 'No way. They might 'mock up' an emergency to examine motives. But NOT poison.'

Perce accepts that, and ploughs on.

'Looks like this game has financial possibilities. Maybe someone who wanted to get the Tournament booking next time? A competitor?'

'That's a possibility.' I didn't mention I'd already considered that motive.

In Perce's style, I'm beginning to appreciate some of Art's qualities. Maybe that's where Art learned to question. For the first time, I'm beginning to have a little respect this man who must still be feeling sick but who is tackling the problem.

The emergency director comes into the ward. 'Who are you? Are you a relative?'

Perce gives a fleeting smile. 'My daughter-in-law'.

'Er, yes. Perce is my father in law. But I'm also Quinn from the café.'

The director flicks thorough the medical reports on clipboards hanging at the bottom of each bed. Mother-in-law Rose who is always quiet, watches him and he smiles reassuringly.

'Most patients will be fine. We've discharged them now. They won't have any long term problems from the poisoning.'

These words reassure me but then I realise he said 'most' not all.

'Guy the chef is in a much more serious state. He's in Intensive Care.'

'Can I visit?'

'Just for five minutes. Check with the nurse.'

The I.C.U. ward has a duty nurse for each patient.

Bea follows me but as she's still so cross with Guy she says, 'You do the talking Quinn.'

When she sees how sick Guy appears, she goes very quiet and hangs back.

Guy has tubes from his arms and face like an outer-space man. Lots of dials and monitors behind him. His bed is raised at an angle. He is bionic man but looks very small under the sheet and the hospital blanket. His breath is laboured but he's determined to explain.

'I'm so sorry about Bea's customers. I was just going to make them a little sick. Not kill anyone.' I realise that he doesn't see Bea behind me. Is his vision affected too?

He chokes a bit. The dials and medical controls and gauges around his bed over-react. The digital graph changes and the lines run up. Frightening.

'Just relax Guy.' We all say stupid things at difficult times. Especially me. How can he relax?

'Broke. Had debts from before. 'Nibbles' suggested it. Wanted the Motives people to move to their venue. Had a bit of a hold over me. Could have pinned the food poisoning charge on me. Salmonella. A batch of bad eggs. Just before I left for overseas.'

The nurse adjusts one of the tubes. I wonder if we should leave but the nurse just nods.

Guy's voice is weak but he continues. ' When I got back a few days ago, they contacted me about the Tournament.'

'Blackmail?' I say. Guy tries to nod but there are too many tubes.

'Smear campaign. Sage Café is getting such a great reputation. It's a threat to others. 'Nibbles' are a bit dodgy. Offered me money to slip something into the food.'

'But WHY did you eat it yourself?'

'Got the amounts wrong. Tasting to check. Hadn't put enough mushrooms in. That's why I made a second batch.'

The nurse indicates it's time for us to go.

'Typical', mutters Bea as we walk to the lifts. 'Ten people poisoned. I should never have...'

I interrupt. 'Luckily most have been released to go home. Art is driving his parents to our place.'

'Has the Health Department finished with my café? Can I go home?'

'Would you rather come to our place?' I offer as the lift arrives and we get in.

'No. I've got to face starting again, as soon as possible.' Bea pushes her blonde hair back and her wan face looks naked.

I hug her and see our reflections in the mirrors of the lift. Why do they put mirrors in hospital lifts? No one looks their best. Then the lift robotic voice says 'Have a nice day. The temperature is...'

'We both look terrible.' Mirror Bea smiles at the mirror-me. 'I've got Dan to worry about too.'

I had wondered why he didn't come with her.

'Emergency just after you phoned me. I'm not sure where he's going. Somewhere dangerous for sure.' Bea shrugs. ' And I can't do a thing about it.'

The robotic lift voice says 'GROUND FLOOR. Enjoy your day.'

'Thankyou we will,' Bea turns to me. 'First sign of mental decline is talking to robots.'

'Giving them a name is the next sign. I yell at my GPS and she's got a name,' I admit.

Bea smiles wryly. 'I was away such a short time, but everything changed here. Dan might be dealing with warfare but a mushroom kills my business. Sounds trivial doesn't it?'

I feel so sorry. How can we save the reputation of her café? Maybe Art can help? We need to get the Motives players back. Xavier might be the answer. I'll seed the idea of a game to him.

'A police report prepared for the coroner but the matter is not subject of a police investigation.' Dr G2 tells us.

Courtesy of Dr Google, all the locals become instant mushroom experts. There are even mushroom jokes. Really bad ones I won't repeat.

Perce corners me. 'I've never been keen on your relationship with my son. But after this weekend I've changed my mind about a few things. And found out about Night Caps. An introduced species. Usually at the bottom of oak trees. Some found in Victorian country towns…The Health department says three people had died from eating death cap mushrooms in past decade and 12 reported cases of poisoning.'

'Sounds like we just added to their stats.'

'Lucky that Guy is recovering.'

Damage control campaign next.

I ring Bea. She needs hope more than anything else.

'I've spoken with Xavier about a possible 'Hypothetical' game. Despite being poisoned in your café, he's keen and he's got considerable money available to invest in games. He was looking for a new project. And he's keen about an idea I suggested inspired by the poisonous mushrooms.'

'What?' Bea doesn't believe me.

'It could be considered research and development in a weird kind of way. ' I say. ' Second suggestion is to tell customers what really happened. They are a bigger part of your market than the Motives players. And they gossip. Art will help you with writing that in a diplomatic way.'

'A media release?'

'Sort of. Motives players are fairly strategic thinkers. They'll side with you. It was a mistake of the competition to imagine that a smear campaign would ruin players' favourite venue. If they work out that this was a kind of blackmail, they'll stay. But they'll want to analyse the motives.'

'What?'

'Xavier is dropping by in the next half hour. Make him a coffee. I'm coming too.'

Bea is very nervous when Xavier arrives. Her hands are

trembling as she makes the coffee, but the big man Xavier is fired up with ideas.

'Not a wasted weekend Bea. Hospital emergency isn't my first choice of locations. No thanks to you. But gave me an idea for a game scenario. D'you reckon Dan would help me with the military details? I've sketched out a game for the next Tournament…the replacement Tournament…as long as you do the catering, no locums. And no mushrooms or fungi.'

We explain the idea I had suggested to Xavier yesterday. He had taken it much further.

'Hypothetically, the scenario is a café in an outer galaxy. An inter-galactic competitor wants to take its business and attempts to smear reputation via contamination in the food, how would they view that? Probably play out the scenario, then decide to stay with Café Sage despite the Health Department warning. A loyal group of fans…and the owner is one of their own… And I've suggested a chemist superhero. But Perce wants to add an industrial espionage angle.'

'Are you going to call the game Night Cap?'

'Maybe.'

I think it might take a bit longer to resurrect the reputation of Bea's Café Sage but Art offered to interview her on Channel Zero. And handle her media free to reduce the damage. Violet is going to chat to her customers.

Guy has agreed to stay away from hospitality and take up other casual work in a nursery. With plants not kids.

'And if the 'Motives' Tournament game can be launched at Café SAGE, that's a start. Could have international interest.'

Bea looks stunned. 'One step at a time. Let's put the OPEN sign back on the door. But I won't be offering a Night Cap drink. We'll stick to coffee and tea and green smoothies.'

Art's live interview from Café Zero will go out tomorrow.

Just enough time for us to help her set up again. Violet arrives with flowers. Mixed yellow and red.

'Yellow for sorrow and red for love. Moving on.'

Quinn's Theory of Time

Einstein's theory of special relativity says that time slows down or speeds up depending on how fast you move relative to something else.

So the time you spend with a lover, seems too short.

Travel fast and time moves more slowly

Or think outside the time barriers.

Time to Kill

I'm running so fast my eyes have floating lights in them. Pinpoints that grow and change colour like a kaleidoscope. My breath is coming in gasps. He's chasing me. I'm not sure how much longer I can keep going. He grabs at me. My elbow is caught. I fall, precisely in the designated spot. Loose gravel crunches as the soles of our sneakers twist, his muscled arms turn me around and he faces the camera with his best angle.

Cut.

'Thanks Quinn. Got it right this time.'

'Okay?' The 'hero' untangles himself from my sweaty limbs. The gravel is hard and leaves an imprint on my left hand which had my full weight pressing down. Little grey, gravelly bits fall off as I rub my hand. We're both still breathing hard.

'Glad we don't have to do that again,' the hero leaves.

The director is happy enough this time. 'Ten minute break'. The film crew leave to grab coffees from the catering van.

I pull myself up and assess the damage. Knees sore. Hand is a bit grazed this time. They should have an excellent shot of the back of my head.

Playing one of the anonymous 'baddie' extras in low budget movie 'Time to Kill' is exhausting, but more varied exercise than going to the gym. I prefer voice-overs. But with our rent due, I take all offers. Auditions are often at very short notice. Occasionally I have to refuse because I have a funeral. A call at 6 pm asking me to go for an audition at 9 am the next morning does happen about once a month. This is for bit-parts and commercials. There is longer lead time with main roles. Important roles are cast first... Little time left to warn actors eligible for smaller roles, like me. Luckily I've never faced the dilemma of being offered an audition for a major role and been forced to reject it because I am conducting a funeral. Maybe one day.

You are usually booked for a minimum of four hours, but it can be longer. If the shoot goes over, you are paid overtime. As a bit-part actor and extra, that's where the good money is... In overtime. But tonight I mustn't be late for the last train.

The actors are a friendly group and there's a bit of overlap at various gigs.

'Good to see you again Quinn.'

I nod. Can't remember his real name. Only that he was a fellow extra in the last shoot and played the non-speaking cab driver.

I glance around at the other part-time actors trying to accumulate credits and cash. A few familiar faces. Some are outstandingly good-looking which requires high maintenance. Like blonde Celeste whose facials, pedicures, manicures, hairdressing, extensions, colouring, tanning, meditation and Pilates classes must cost more than she earns. But she has fabulous cheek bones! And a sense of fun. Luckily I specialise in character parts, partly because I enjoy the dressing up. Other times, like today, I'm just an extra, one of the background ones who don't speak. Low maintenance. Next step up are bit-parts where you get one or two lines. My highest paid job was actually just for my hands. It was a commercial, last year and I had to put together a wooden puzzle. They gave me a manicure as part of the job. That was fun.

The extras enjoy chatting in between takes. Waiting is

the norm for actors. A bit like weddings and late brides and celebrants having to be patient. LOTS of waiting around. I usually read or write in the green room. As an extra or bit-part actor, it is not unusual to wait around for more than four hours until they are ready for your fifteen minutes on set.

As I wipe my sweaty face, Celeste shows me her latest business card. 'What do you think Quinn?' Celeste asks, with a grin. Her face has been air–brushed on the card.

Unnecessary. She looked great before.

"A work of art," I say and check the words.

'Celestial Perfection?' That's a fake name isn't it? Award-winning actor? Which award? 'If you submit clips of your work for obscure, minor awards, you can claim you've been acknowledged even if those in the business, know you probably paid the entry fee and did the listing yourself.

Celeste smiles and the cheekbones show. 'Mostly they don't ask. If they do, I say I was long listed. And Celestial Perfection IS my real name. My parents' choice. You have to be memorable for something. Celeste is the name friends use. I don't mind you still calling me that.'

'It's shorter, Celeste.' Not the moment to mention I offer naming ceremonies.

Maybe I should update my business card?

'Quinn, the Celebrant Sleuth specialising in wedding, funerals and solving mysteries,' could be replaced by…'Time to Kill' actor specialising in 'baddies on the run.' And naming ceremonies for aspiring actors.'

Is fiction on business cards, fraud or survival?

Quinn's Law of Business Cards

No face-lifts of facts by faction or fiction. And photo I.D. on business card should be within a year of the real face.

Not much work lately. The fee-paying kind, not cosmetic

surgery. Although around me, there are a few actors who have trouble doing the range of expressions due to face-work.

If this were the last day of my life, is this how I want to spend it? Playing a 'baddie' actor? Temporary diversion. I'd rather be with Art at home, but that's not possible today.

One bonus! Catering is great at the caravan on set. They feed us well. The crew come back for second helpings. Sausages. Wraps. Hot chocolate. Banana bread slices. I only want liquid after rehearsing that run so many times, but I like looking at the foody options steaming in the easily portable containers. Maybe this is the kind of catering Bea could do if SAGE doesn't recover.

Some of the Tournament people have returned and a few of the locals, but Bea is struggling financially. SAGE café hasn't recovered from the death cap poisoning incident. Killed Sage's reputation and halved Bea's income.

'Unless I can earn more, I'll have to close in a couple of months.' Bea confided yesterday. 'The lease is due for renewal then.'

'What about investors?'

'Who would invest in a failing café?'

The only person I know with any spare money is Art's father Perce. But I'm not in a position to ask him for any favours.

Eating helps fill in the time between takes. On the set, others knit which is the latest crafty hobby, chat, fill in puzzles, or catch up on social media. Often I write eulogies or plan wedding services. But not today.

This has been a rare week with no weddings and no funerals. Part-time acting pays some bills, but often they are low budget movies with very slow invoices. Luckily, Billee gets me work via her agency, but often I have to drive to the city for the studio jobs. Makes it a long day.

'Might have to hang around a bit on this 'Time to Kill' job,' Billee warns. Really appreciate having her as an agent and a bit of emotional support. Then I realize she's joking.

'Time to Kill' Oh, I get it.'

'You're a bit slow today Quinn,' says Billee. 'Wake up.'

I decide to catch the train to avoid the cost of city parking, especially when unsure how long we'll be on the set which is a cobbled back- lane leading to an urban park with gravelly patches in a playground and dis-used warehouses behind. Kids have been banned from using the swings and slides while we're filming. Low budget thriller with some scary makeup effects with lots of fake blood. Enough to thrill any kid. I still haven't got used to seeing costumed 'characters' wandering around ordinary settings. Nothing like seeing a ghoulishly made-up zombie sipping coffee at the catering van while checking his messages.

I check mine. Train cancellation.

In a small country town, locals know every train and bus arrival. Mostly they're spot on BUT tonight my train home 6.03 ex Melbourne has been cancelled. It's the last one. So I'll have to get the earlier 5.33.

Art's involved with his new partner at our place until 7 pm, our agreed time. So I don't want to be home unexpectedly early tonight. Time to kill.

ॐ

Officially, Art and I are now in a poly relationship – he has a second partner Dee with whom he gets to enjoy the physical stuff that I'm not interested in, while I get to stop worrying about depriving him of something he wants (he's always been very reassuring about that, but it's hard not to feel guilty when I know he's not ace himself). Ace is asexual. Someone who does not experience sexual attraction to anyone. That's me. But I can still have romantic feelings and I do care about Art.

It's the first time we've tried this arrangement, but they've been together for well over a month and it has gone very well so far – not entirely without hitches, as no relationship is (let alone a three-way one), but we have been able to build something still loving and caring. Though the other partner Dee and I are not technically in a relationship, we are friendly – not necessarily a must in a situation like this, but I think it helps a lot with building trust. I said 'Yes,' when he asked me but now it's real and I've met Dee a few times, I'm not sure about the future. Will she continue to feel their arrangement is sexual only with no emotional attachment? At the moment, despite the sex, she sees Art as a kind of political or social experiment. No, that's unkind. It's just the two of them together. I'm not involved physically. The first time I noticed her was with the Sunday cyclists at Bea's café. But Art had met her before. She is his choice, but I haven't asked his reasons. She must be able to keep her life in discreet compartments or it won't work.

She's younger. A lot younger. And much taller than Art. Most people are, but she has the advantage of being new. I'm too familiar. And ordinary. And not interested in sex. Even if I have tried. But Art and I share ideas, company, a home and a life and we're long term partners. Dee does not live with us. He just meets with her occasionally.

I know rural areas have a reputation for being less tolerant, but I'd like to think that our town could be accepting of a non-standard relationship among people they know and like. But I'm a bit scared to share our news, so we're keeping it a secret. Dee agreed to that at my request. Hope she keeps her promise. Unsure how I could enforce that promise, if I had to. Anyway, she has her other life.

ॐ

Just as this last country train for the night is leaving at 5.33, Violet arrives, seconds before the automatic doors close. She's laden with designer bags, a coat, a long scarf on which she trips and a glossy magazine.

'You cut that fine. Did you know the later train was cancelled?' I say, picking up her mobile which she dropped as she fell into the seat next to me.

Violet nods and indicates the magazine cover. 'In town because I've just won the award. Can call myself an award-winning florist now.'

I glance at the florist shop on the magazine cover. It looks familiar. 'Infinity Blooms?'

'Mm.'

'And have you been invited on the TV Eccentrics program yet? You must have 100 watering cans by now?'

Violet shakes her head. 'I have 101 cans. Zac counted them. Only problem was the producers wanted to know about my past life, for a feature. Can you believe it?' 'Actually Art showed me the media release at Channel Zero.' I admit. Before he told me about today's appointment with Dee. I prefer to call her that rather than girlfriend or …lover or …therapist. I've suggested they meet at our place because a motel would be expensive, which Art can't afford and would make him feel more obliged to me for taking money from our combined budget, so I try to give them space.

Gossip travels fast in our town, and motels are very public. I didn't mention that.' Who is interviewing you?'

'WEDDING Magazine. They've got links with the TV network. And a few bloggers.' Violet is scrolling down her phone. She gasps. Her face turns so pale that old freckles re-appear on her cheeks. Her neck is wrinkled. Her fingers tremble as she tries to re-trace the digital link.

'Bloody hell. Why do these things never work when you want them. That Stella blogger is calling me a killer.'

'What?' I remember Cousin Stella from the Football Hall of Fame wedding. The one with the face jewellery. And a desire to know everything. And share it all, online.

'Why has Stella got you on her blog screen?'

'She's one of the freelancers who cover media stories. I was SO thrilled at first. But now she wants to write a story about my past.'

'That's good isn't it?'

'It depends how far in the past. I just wanted to limit the story to my country life now. She says I killed my husband. And that's the angle. Not the flowers. Or the eccentric watering cans décor. But she hasn't written the article yet. Or even interviewed me. Just put out the teaser heading.'

Violet looks defeated. I pick up the WEDDING magazine, 'Featured florist for next month? The Mysterious Shrinking Shady Violet who has a PAST!'

' Violet isn't even my real name.'

'That's defamation isn't it, if she calls you a killer? Unless it is true?'

'It IS true. It was an accident. I was imprisoned for manslaughter. Ten years ago. That's why I came here. And changed my name.'

So when Violet had said earlier that her marriage had ended, she wasn't telling a lie. The husband was dead.

I can imagine what Cousin Stella might write about our

poly relationship. Sensational is the norm for Stella. She overdoses on exclamation marks and caps in bold.

'Why did you change your name to Violet?'

'Sounds more like a florist.'

'Any other reason?'

'Didn't want people from my old life finding me. Before the trial. I'd always been fairly shy and my husband was VERY controlling. He said I was stupid and I believed him, partly because of the spelling. So, I always kept in the background. Then I had a birthday and felt my life was nearly over. I decided to become the person I wanted to be for the rest of my life, somewhere new that didn't know I was shy.'

'Like acting a role?'

'Like becoming the role. The Florist, that's what I wanted to be. Not the Battered Wife. But I ended up being labelled a Killer. I didn't intend to kill anyone. My husband attacked me when I tried to leave quietly. My bags were packed. He completely lost it and pinned me on the kitchen floor. I hit him with the iron. It was on the highest setting. It sprayed. He slipped, hit his head and died. I was charged with manslaughter and went to prison.'

Her voice was flat as if she was reciting a news bulletin. Amazing that Violet had never told me anything of this before. And she had not told anyone else either. Amazing for someone known as the local gossip.

'If you're featured on national media, it's likely that someone from your past might recognize you,' I warn her.

'Make-up, hair and different clothes and name make it easier for a woman to change.

I had a different surname back then. Dunn is my 'chosen' name now.'

I think of Celeste's business card.

'We all have secrets,' I say.

'So what's your secret Quinn? It won't be a secret anymore if you tell me.'

Violet was NOT stupid.

Is our country town ready for our secrets? Maybe Violet and I should just swap but tell no-one else? Like that Strangers on a Train movie...kill the other person's reputation...by proxy. But Infinity Blooms is gossip centre extraordinaire.

I take a deep breath.

'D'you think they could cope with a convicted murderer and polyamory where we live? Country is a bit slower than city.'

'Poly-what?' Violet frowns.

'Adultery is different. In polyamory, the partners know about each other.'

'You and Art and what's-her-name?'

'Dee.'

'No. Doesn't matter what fancy label you use. Poly whatever. You might think you know your partner. Or partners. Locals think they know us. Not the same thing. Like I thought I knew my husband. I didn't. And he thought he knew me. But he made a mistake. And so did I. The difference is I have a chance to change things now.'

Killing a Reputation

Cousin Stella is still on my contacts list from our Hall of Football Fame wedding. And her honeymooner cousins are continuing to winter in Antarctica, isolated on their ice-bound expedition. The court case for co-murderers Great Uncle Peter and Joseph was postponed, again, on grounds of ill-health. Expensive lawyers. My bet is wily Great Uncle Peter will probably have a funeral before he faces any judge in a court room. That's one ceremony I don't want to perform.

Should I Skype Stella? Not yet. I'll investigate her methods first. Might need Art's digital help with that. And find some way I can convince Stella NOT to kill Violet's reputation and her 'Infinity Blooms' business.

Claud likes new ways to attract clients to Everest. He loves putting together ideas which have not been in that combination before. He grabs me as I leave legal documents to be signed at the Everest office. Claud is wearing overalls and has his tool kit with him. 'Plumbing emergency,' he explains as he takes off the overalls and reveals his 'grey manager trousers ' underneath. He puts on his suit jacket and the Everest blue lanyard around his neck with the I.D. Manager Claud in dark font big enough for sight- challenged residents to read. 'Fixed the blocked toilet in No 24.' Neatly he packs his ex-tradie tools ready for the next time.

Flora chose well in appointing Claud. Wonder if Ed

appreciates the legacy his mother left. Claud talks as he fixes his tasteful blue tie. 'Seniors' Week' is coming up. Most of our residents are senior seniors. And if that WEDDING magazine is coming, how about a quick ceremony at Everest's Chapel on the day? As background? With Violet's flowers from 'Infinity Blooms'. She supplies the Village with flowers weekly anyway. Good publicity for both of us for a change. I suspect he does know about Violet's past. And is trying to 'fix' stuff.

'Anybody in mind as a bride? Or groom? Do you mean a real wedding or models? Actors?' I ask. 'Short notice for a wedding. You know how long the paperwork takes.' I nod towards his overflowing desk. He takes such good care of his tools, but papers are a different priority.

Claud smiles.' Action first, paperwork later. I wasn't thinking of having a funeral. Just wanting our Chapel as the setting. Could have a re-commitment ceremony if you prefer?'

Was Claud getting personal?

'Art and I are not in your age demographic. And I can't marry myself. I'm not a ventriloquist's dummy.'

Claud smiles wryly. 'Running Everest is getting harder. We really miss Flora. I used to ask her advice a lot. Other residential villages have had financial problems plastered all over the media and it doesn't help us. Too many deaths in the news.'

Has he seen Stella's first promo about the Shady Violet? Gossip travels fast in a country town but not all are digital natives who read their news only online. On the other hand, maybe he is just mentioning the lingering effects of Flora's death by misadventure? Or Rocky's death at the Barefoot Bowls? There are more places left vacant in the village than ever before. And Claud's main job is to keep the business running.

'See you later Quinn. Today I have to finalise getting those rock sculptures out of Rocky's front garden, or we'll never get anyone interested in that property. And repaint the front sign so it no longer says Ever-Rest. Bye.'

৵

Under Violet's instructions, Zac is arranging blooms in pots outside 'Infinity Blooms'. The deep red, yellow and orange flowers add colour to the street, where a couple of 'grey-ish' shops have recent CLOSING DOWN END OF LEASE SALE signs on their windows and no life inside.

'Vacant shops don't help. We all have cash flow problems in this street.' Worried, Violet mutters to me. 'Can just imagine Stella's title in big letters on the next blog. No-one will miss it. EX-KILLER drives business away in her street.'

'I don't think so,' I reassure quietly so Zac can't hear. 'I Skyped Stella for a chat. About the legal consequences of defamation. Publication of untrue material that could lead an ordinary, reasonable person to think less of you. On Facebook comments, Twitter and email. AND this includes Cousin Stella's blogging.'

'How did she respond?'

'She said "Piss off!" And switched off.' Violet's eyebrows go up. ' I did kill him. What she said was true. But it was the way she wrote it. And the heading! He died but I didn't murder him. It was accidental.'

'I realize that. So I rang back. Before Stella hung up again, I pointed out that she had got the obscenely highly paid, Wedding Magazine job to write about YOU as a Shady Violet Murderess who killed her husband by providing examples of

HER earlier published work from your original trial. BUT that court story was fraudulent. Pirated! Stella wasn't there. It had been written by someone else. She plagiarized and presented another investigative crime journalist's work as her own. She did fake it. And you weren't even called Violet then. And so, if I wrote on social media about Stella's fraudulent CV, it was NOT defamation, because it was true. For a freelancer, reputation matters for future paid work.'

'Would you?'

'Probably not. But she can't risk it. Especially as I attached the file to prove I had the original documents written by the other journalist. And indicated the chunks she lifted. And then I hung up on her.'

Violet looks overwhelmed. And so am I by Art's research skills. He helped me find Stella's fake digital history of supposed expertise. So helpful to have a live-in sleuth and especially one who feels emotionally a little indebted. Art has been so attentive since Dee became part of his other life. But that's ok. I love him and am glad when he is happy. A TV camera crew is due to arrive in ten minutes to film 'Infinity Blooms' as a 'Wedding Magazine' flower feature. Focusing on the 101 watering cans as signs of eccentric collections and regional design. And then to go onto Everest's Chapel after lunch, to film the re-commitment vows of the 90 year old Angelos from the nursing home, married for 70 years. With me conducting the ceremony. Rent-a-crowd will be there too. Scones, jam and clotted cream ordered from SAGE catering. Claud has been busy. Plumbing wasn't the only thing he fixed.

Meanwhile Violet is still apprehensive about what might be said in public which would destroy 'Infinity Blooms' and her local reputation.

'I went to court because my husband's death was due to

me. And then to prison, that's true,' Violet admits. 'Stella wrote that on her first blog promo.'

'But it wasn't murder. The court said it was 'Manslaughter'. ' Not the moment to mention to spelling- challenged Violet that man's laughter AND man slaughter use the same words, just the spaces and meanings are different. Not relevant. Just linguistically interesting to word-freaks like me. And to crossword and riddle enthusiasts.

Meanwhile, in the street, Dr G2's pharmacy is busy with customers seeking prescriptions and on the wall of the florist shop, the 101 watering cans rattle in the wind. 'Infinity Blooms' is a riot of colour inside, floral scents with strategically placed flowers and quirky labels. A haven of damp perfume and positioned colour. Dark to light green. Lemon to gold. Photographs from grateful bridal customers and testimonials. Her sample love poems are on the wall. I check the spelling for Violet, and quietly fix up a couple. Violet catches me.

'OK? Look all right on screen now…the spelling?'

I nod. ' Look what Zac's managed outside.'

Zac stands back and looks at his floral arrangement with what would be pride but 18 year olds don't admit satisfaction with work that someone else had told them to do.

'Infinity Blooms' spelled in blooming, tiny pots of colour. Pansies. Lilies of the Valley. Forget-me-nots and flowers I don't know. KAT sits alongside purring approval.

'Thanks Zac. But I still don't want you delivering flowers to Everest Chapel on the trike, yet,' says Violet.

'Maybe I could paint numbers on the watering cans, then they'd know how many?' offers Zac.

'A few more important jobs first. Can you sweep the street either side too? Move the bin to cover that graffiti.'

Violet goes inside to tidy up, just in case the TV crew come early, and Zac writes an APOLOGY POTPLANT sign, and adds 'HALF PRICE TODAY ONLY.'

'Recognise that pot plant Quinn. Didn't you give one to Rose?' Perce smiles as he passes on his way to SAGE café. 'Half an apology now?'

He looks a typical Grey Nomad in those drip dry beige shorts, retirees favour, but I know not to judge by his appearance. Perce is a shrewd businessman on a mission. Revitalised, he seems to be enjoying a sense of purpose instead of 'filling in' time.

'Bea told me. About her business problems. Not enough customers.' Perce is searching online via his phone. 'Bea's got three options. Either get more customers or cut her costs. Or value-add.'

'Oh.'

'All country towns are doing it hard. Just checking who owns these shops. Leases are nearly up.' Perce gestures towards 'Infinity Blooms' and then to SAGE café.

'Looks colourful with the lime-green branding. Well cared for. Cheerful. No graffiti. Wonderful food. She built it up so well the first time, but that night-cap poisoning has been devastating on the café's reputation.'

'And...'

'Both have big floor space they are not using. Flowers and food could go together. Could give it new life if they joined up. Value adding.'

'Violet and Bea? Infinity Blooms with SAGE café?'

'Why not? Rent is a big cost. They both live in flats behind their shops. Would cut accommodation costs too.'

I think of Bea's very basic unit with the sagging spare bed

behind the café. Not sure if Violet would fit there. Or if she would want to try.

'But what about the timing? If the TV people are coming today. They'll be filming 'Infinity Blooms' in this shop. With this address.'

'Ah!' Perce has found what he's looking for on his screen. 'Now that's a turn-up. Owned by Everest. Nominee Edward Nat. Do you know him?'

'Er, yes. Flora's son. Must have inherited it. I don't think Bea knew Ed was her landlord. Nor Violet. Probably hidden via various company names.'

I step inside the florist shop and call out to Violet who is in the flat out the back getting changed. There are two bedrooms, and it's bigger than the café flat so maybe they could share? Violet also has a better taste in furniture but Bea can cook. Sage Café has lots of fittings. Could they all be transferred?

'Violet, did you know Ed owned your shop now?'

Violet's voice is matter-of-fact. 'I knew one of Flora's companies owned it before. Zac used to joke that maybe one day he'd be my boss. And that I should let him ride my trike because he liked it so much that one day he'd run the company. Ed is his uncle.'

'Of course.' Ed is not one of my favourites. I don't think Ed is stupid. Just lazy. And cunning. But occasionally he makes a mistake. Like recently mentioning to Art about being in Flora's garage on the night of her death. Suspicious but nothing we can prove. What kind of man would let his nephew assume the guilt of Flora's death? And now his maternal meal ticket has gone, Ed is using up assets with as little effort on his part as he can manage. But he irritates Art even more.

'Making a virtue out of not learning new skills, is not

charming: just stupidity. He says he doesn't respond to e-mail. Just got to press the button. Not rocket science.'

Art has firm views on technological idiots. 'If you don't know, ask. Don't pretend you are superior because you insist on doing things the old way. Or not at all.'

Now is not the moment to suggest to Violet that SAGE catering could move into her florist shop. Especially as she is getting so much wonderful publicity in connection with the Wedding T.V. But she does have enough plumbing, electrical and cooking connections to share. I check.

One slight complication: KAT the territorial cat who may not welcome a newcomer.

Then I remember another, bigger complication. Dan! He might be on a secret military mission, but he does come home at short notice and will expect to share a bed with his wife. Three sharing behind the shop may not be viable in this street.

ॐ

Decisively, Violet emerges from the shop, with fresh makeup and a violet coloured apron around her stout middle with 'Infinity Blooms' embroidered in black on it. She hands a similar apron to Zac.

'Zac, take down that Half Price sign on the Apology Potplants. We don't want them to think we are cheap. Or going out of business. Even if I do have cash flow problems. Don't apologise for anything. Wear this.'

Zac's face falls. 'A sort of purple apron!'

'It's violet. Sort of …isn't close enough. Don't you know the difference in your purples yet. Have you any idea how many shades of purple exist? Part of this job is to learn your colours…and the more obscure names. The popular shades of purple are Amethyst, Fuchsia, Lavender, Lilac, Magenta, Mauve, Orchid, Thistle and Violet.'

I'm impressed with Violet's knowledge but also her rise in confidence. 'Thistle is a colour?'

'Whatever,' says Zac.

'Then you can ride the trike to deliver the re-commitment flowers to the Chapel for the cameras. And arrange them. I've sketched the design. Keep to it. I need to stay here for the television people.'

Reluctantly Zac puts the apron on and accepts the design paper. He looks like a skinny, bony insect in an over-sized skin.

Ed Nat slouches down the street. His hair needs a trim and his stubble is speckled grey. The trackie pants could have been sleepwear. Looks like he just fell out of bed.

'So Quinn, you're still hatching, matching and dispatching?' he sneers.

Ed has a charm bypass.

If anyone else said that in any other tone, it might almost be acceptable. Ed always made me feel like retreating rapidly. But I try a polite strategy. 'Ed, have you met Perce, my father in law who wanted to meet you?'

'G'day. Are you the one who rang me about the lease? '

'Yes. Just checking on when it expires.' Perce scrolls through his digital notes.

'End of this month. Rent will double then. Why, did you want to lease a shop?'

'No,' says Perce. 'But after the celebration is on television and in the Wedding Magazine, Violet and Bea might want to re-negotiate their leases. More customers may come to this street.'

સ&

'No, I don't want to lose their rent. If they go in together, I lose one lease.' Ed blusters.

Perce looks down the street. Quite a few empty shops. 'If you don't agree to that, you might lose both of them. Surely you're better off with one busy shop and regular rent than vacant dwellings and graffiti.'

'You can do what you like as long as some rent is paid. I don't care whose name is on the lease as long as I get the money.' Ed has lost interest in business for the day. Short attention span. He leaves.

'Great story,' says the director as he left. 'And just loved the rocks sculpture too. Claud explained to us it was a new form of therapy for residents.'

I look at Claud. He just smiles.

The T.V. crew has gone and we're all happy but exhausted after a highly successful event at the Chapel. Even the ninety-something Angelos are napping after too much afternoon tea and star status.

Back at the shops, I explain to Bea. 'Stella has been unethical, using publishing credits she didn't have, to get the job with the magazine. And she's threatening to kill Violet's reputation by writing about her past. Victim of domestic violence and she finally hit back at her husband. Charged with manslaughter and went to prison. Came here to start a new life.'

Bea nods and the light glints on her blonde streaks 'Suspected that. Have you managed to block Stella from writing about her as a Killer?'

'Yes. And offered her an alternative subject. Collaborative businesses in regional areas. Female rural enterprises. Doubt if she'll follow that up.'

'Well it is happening around here. Perce suggested Violet and I share one shop space. Halve our rent for the next year. Then he'd be prepared to invest in the café as a silent partner.'

Unsure how silent Perce might be, but it's a new start for Bea.

'What would you call it?'

We stop in front of 'Infinity Blooms'.

'Infinity Blooms Sagely?'

'Sage Blooms?'

'Infinity was Art's suggestion. Never-ending work.'

We laugh. 'Your Art is so helpful. He offered to make a Sage's Café cooking doco for Youtube. Sort of documentary journey of growing fruit and vegetables and making them into preserves and jams. The site would have recipes and an online shop for purchases. Most would be gluten-free to cater for food allergies and a number of stories would relate to living with Coeliac disease,' says Bea.

'You haven't got Coeliac! Or any of the other allergies or food issues.'

'Customers have. So it makes sense to cater for those markets.'

'Could I be an apprentice?' Zac interrupts.

'With me?' queries Violet. 'Not sure how KAT would react. She's the Boss around here.'

'With Sage Café AND 'Infinity Blooms'. When you move in together?'

Violet objects. 'Haven't decided. What about my goldfish tank? Can't have that alongside Bea cooking fish?'

'I'm not sure how we'd manage in the same shop.

Sometimes I like to get away from people. Unlike customers, you don't have to talk to flowers. But sometimes I do,' Violet admits.

'I know how you feel,' Bea admits. 'Let's agree on our own spaces. But Sage Infinity might work. We have a week or so to think about it. '

That night, over dinner and a glass of wine, Art shares his news with me. Perce is considering making Ed an offer for the freehold on the two shops and maybe another in-between. 'Expansion with a silent partner.'

'Will Perce be silent?'

Art smiled. 'No, but…he will inject cash. Dad drives a hard bargain and Ed just wants money with no effort attached. I think the real reason is Perce is bored without a business to run and he's given up on me. This way Bea and Violet could each stay in their own shops and Perce would have a reason to give advice without being called 'interfering'.

Art then makes a suggestion to me too.

'Maybe you'd like to have a commitment service for us?'

'You and Dee?'

'No, you and me. When I watched the re-commitment service you did with the ninety-something couple, it made me think. I wonder if we'll last that long?'

'We'd have to live to over 100. They started a bit earlier than us. Besides I can't marry myself. But I'll think about it.'

Quinn's Variation 3 on $E = mc^2$

Emotion = relationship multiplied by commitment doubled, regardless of numbers involved.

A Sort of Appendix
Quinn's Theories
of Relativity

Most people only know Albert Einstein from t-shirt quotes, but … I admit I occasionally adapt his 'Theory of…' quotes for funerals or weddings. Not really plagiarism because I always mention Einstein, just an updated tribute to the most significant science philosopher (in my opinion). One of my heroes and gives a bit of gravitas to a service.

Quinn's Theory of Relativity
The likelihood of the relationship ending in divorce is directly related to the number of arguments during rehearsals, obsessive preparation and the bride's budget on self.

Quinn's Law of Hijacking Grief
When a neighbour or distant relative feels entitled to claim greater loss and more sympathy than the bereaved partner who is too polite to contradict. Also known as Enjoying Funerals at Others' Cost.

Quinn's Theory of 'Stuff Ups'
The most incomprehensible thing about the world is that it is comprehensible.'– is my all purpose Albert Einstein quote to explain any 'stuff-up'.

Quinn's Problem Law of Q&A

Sometimes it's about knowing which is the right question to ask. Q& A is about problem-identifying not just solving a mystery. And knowing when to shut up!

Quinn's Grave Theory

Ignore grave threats of everlasting revenge by an Ex-spouse. Haunting penalties are difficult to administer in chargeable minutes AFTER a funeral.

Quinn's Theory of Attraction

A Romance Detector finds romance rather like a metal detector seeks gold- and can be observed in action when two people exert a force of attraction on one another and they are drawn to Romance.

Quinn's Law of Naming

When choosing a baby name, know that you'll inadvertently insult all those whose choice of name is NOT used. Remember future form- filling and do not include ALL relatives names or multiple hyphens in surname. Only guarantee : the recipient of the name will hate it as a teenager or even before.

Quinn's Theory of Funeral Secrets

At a funeral, we acknowledge the life of the person and maybe the many identities, actions and secret lives of which the family and friends were unaware. For some a shock, for others a relief.

Quinn's Theory of Soul-Mates

The number of times the word soul-mates is used in public is in reverse proportion to the number of months the relationship lasts.

The Time of Quinn
Einstein's theory of special relativity says that time slows down or speeds up depending on how fast you move relative to something else
So the time you spend with a partner/ lover, seems too short. Travel fast and time moves more slowly.

Quinn's Variation on E = mc²
Emotion = marriage multiplied by commitment doubled.
Theory of special relativity is Einstein's famous equation E = mc². In this formula E is energy, m is mass, and c is the constant speed of light. An interesting result of this equation is that energy and mass are related.

Quinn's Law of Business Cards.
No face-lifts of facts by faction or fiction. And photo I.D. on business card should be within a year of the real face.

Quinn's Variation 3 on E = mc²
Emotion = relationship multiplied by commitment doubled, regardless of numbers involved.

Acknowledgements

With acknowledgement to the many celebrants who generously shared their experiences with me and to Sally Cant who trains celebrants. And thanks to Hespa for helping with the asexuality research and to George Ivanoff for actor research. With gratitude to my first readers Rosemary Brown, Susanne Gervay, Pauline Luke and Nancy Hogan. This is a work of fiction.

www.ingramcontent.com/pod-product-compliance
Lightning Source LLC
Chambersburg PA
CBHW070443260626
47161CB00004B/1190